DEADLY NIGHTSHADE

Also edited by Peter Haining:

NIGHTFRIGHTS
THE MONSTER MAKERS
THE GHOST'S COMPANION

DEADLY NIGHTSHADE

Strange Tales of the Dark

Edited by

PETER HAINING

TAPLINGER PUBLISHING COMPANY
NEW YORK

Published in the United States in 1978 by
TAPLINGER PUBLISHING CO., INC.
New York, New York

Selection and original material
Copyright © 1977 by Peter Haining
All rights reserved. Printed in the U.S.A.

No part of this book may be reproduced or transmitted in any form or by any means, electronic or mechanical, including photocopy, recording, or any information storage and retrieval system now known or to be invented, without permission in writing from the publisher, except by a reviewer who wishes to quote brief passages for inclusion in a magazine, newspaper, or broadcast

Library of Congress Cataloging in Publication Data

Main entry under title:

Deadly nightshade.

1. Horror tales, American. 2. Horror tales, English. 3. Children—Fiction. I. Haining, Peter.
PZ1.D33 [PS648.H6] 823'.0872 77-92767
ISBN 0-8008-2123-8

For my nephew Christopher

Contents

	page
Editor's Introduction	7
Lost Hearts *M. R. James*	11
The Doll's Ghost *Francis Marion Crawford*	23
Nurse's Tale *H. R. Wakefield*	37
The Attic *Algernon Blackwood*	46
The Thing in the Cellar *David H. Keller*	53
The Dabblers *W. F. Harvey*	61
The Tortoise-Shell Cat *Greye La Spina*	71
The Looking-Glass Tree *Joan Aiken*	87
The Human Angle *William Tenn*	108
Gabriel-Ernest *Saki*	114
Sweets to the Sweet *Robert Bloch*	122
The Witch of Ramoth *Mark Van Doren*	132
Twilight Play *August Derleth*	139
Mr Lupescu *Anthony Boucher*	148
Silent Snow, Secret Snow *Conrad Aiken*	153
Midnight Express *Alfred Noyes*	174
The October Game *Ray Bradbury*	180
Acknowledgements	190

Editor's Introduction

I can still remember quite clearly the first horror story I ever heard, although the occasion was well over a quarter of a century ago. The tale was very short, very strange and it sent a shiver coursing up my spine! On reflection, I realise that it was one of the reasons why the chilling story—the story of fear—has become such a favourite of mine: and why I have continued to search for other stories as good as it was, or, if possible, even better. I have to admit that among all the others I now like, I have never found another quite so effectively short or one that remains so clearly in the mind full of horrid possibilities.

Let me therefore recall the story for you just as it was told to me before a roaring fire one winter's eve. The teller was an old Scottish relative and I can hear his voice rising distinctly just above the crack and spit of the logs burning in the grate:

'A man wakes up suddenly in his bed in the middle of the night,' my relative says. 'He has the feeling that there is something in the room with him. He reaches out for the matches to light his candle and reassure himself. And, without a sound, the box is *placed* in his hand . . .'

Superb, isn't it—and so eerie! What could it possibly be —man or beast or spirit? Whatever it is, there can be no doubting it is clever and perfectly at home in the dark! These considerations apart, we can see in those few words all the elements of the best horror story. The ordinary situation, the predictable human reaction, and the inexplicable happening in the darkness. No more need be added: the mind, every mind, will have its own idea about the climax.

My delight in this particular story had led me to enjoy other stories set at night, under the cover of darkness—the very hours of horror, in fact. For is not the mind at its most active at this time; most able to see and hear things never associated with daylight?

Superstition, that inheritance from our primitive past, will make much of the darkness, of course, and make us believe in all manner of impossible things. But should we be unduly perturbed about wanting to experience such things? I think not—for a scare floods the body with relief when the truth emerges and fright turns to laughter when something quite innocuous proves the real cause. And relief and laughter never did anyone I know any harm!

It has been with that first horror story in mind that I have put together this new collection. For the tales in *Deadly Nightshade* are all about strangeness in the dark; and they are also all about children in one way or another—just as I was when I had my first brush with the unknown.

We all have a mysterious experience at some time in our lives—something we can never quite explain—but it is undoubtedly more deeply felt and certainly seen with less prejudice when we are young. And that makes for a rather special kind of encounter, I have always felt.

My contributors to this book are of a similar mind, too, and through the eyes of the young have opened up a whole new world of strangeness that might be difficult to encompass in any other kind of collection. Interestingly, quite a number of their stories are based on unusual experiences they themselves had as children.

All the traditional figures of the horror story are here—ghosts, vampires, werewolves, witches, monsters and so on—but the introduction of children adds a whole new element. For we can never be quite sure how they will react under the circumstances.

I like to think that the stories I have selected are all ones that the reader will be able to relate to in some way. Oh, yes, he may be able to say, something like that has happened to me. Or, yes, I know just how that character feels and why he is behaving that way. Although, let me hasten to add, I don't think he will quite want to identify with all the youngsters herein, for one or two have some very strange traits!

All the stories in the collection were written in this century and I have done this primarily because in so many of the old tales not a great deal happens and even if the atmosphere and characters are well described, there is usually a let-down at the end when everything is explained logically. I like to let my imagination roam free when reading a story of this kind—and be in for a real surprise when I reach the last page!

Of course different things affect different people, and I was reading only the other day that one of the greatest puzzles to psychologists is why one child can read ghost stories without being the least disturbed while another cannot bear to even have the book in the same room. Yet, added the report, both these children will agree that Blind Pew in *Treasure Island* is the most terrifying character in fiction.

The simple answer to this dilemma is that we don't know why anyone will react in a certain way to a story or situation. Or why we should even be surprised at the idea of someone or something handing us a box of matches in the dark.

It is, though, the reason why stories of fright can always weave their particular magic on a large number of us, and in this belief I now commend to you the following assembly of tales. I think they all have the special feel of what it is like to be young, imaginative . . . and alone in the dark.

PETER HAINING
January 1977

Lost Hearts

M. R. JAMES

Probably the first kind of object we think about in connection with strange happenings in the dark is a ghost. Certainly there are a great many stories of apparitions and, like me, you may even know of someone who says they have actually seen one. Whether you happen to believe in them or not—and over the years there have been a lot of ordinary, sensible people who are absolutely convinced they have seen something—there is no disputing that they make very good topics for stories. There is also very little argument that few authors have written about them with more conviction and thrilling effect than M. R. James, who was certainly a serious-minded, scholarly gentleman. Professor James was for some years the Provost of Eton College and used to delight (not to mention quite frighten, I understand) groups of his pupils by reading them stories about the supernatural which he had himself written. Today these tales are regarded as classics of their kind, and there could hardly be a more suitable way to begin this book than with one of them. "Lost Hearts" is all about an orphan boy who is taken into the household of a mysterious relative and what befalls them both in the depths of night . . .

It was, as far as I can ascertain, in September of the year 1811 that a post-chaise drew up before the door of Aswarby Hall, in the heart of Lincolnshire. The little boy who was the only passenger in the chaise, and who jumped out as soon as it had stopped, looked about him with the keenest curiosity during the short interval that elapsed between the ringing of the bell and the opening of the hall door. He saw a tall, square, red-brick house, built in the reign of Anne; a stone-pillared porch had been added in the purer classical style of 1790; the windows of the house were many, tall and narrow, with small panes and thick white woodwork. A pediment, pierced with a round window, crowned the front. There were wings to right and left, connected by curious glazed galleries, supported by colonnades, with the central block. These wings plainly contained the stables and offices of the house. Each was surmounted by an ornamental cupola with a gilded vane.

An evening light shone on the building, making the window-panes glow like so many fires. Away from the Hall in front stretched a flat park studded with oaks and fringed with firs, which stood out against the sky. The clock in the church-tower, buried in trees on the edge of the park, only its golden weather-cock catching the light, was striking six, and the sound came gently beating down the wind. It was altogether a pleasant impression, though tinged with the sort of melancholy appropriate to an evening in early autumn, that was conveyed to the mind of the boy who was standing in the porch waiting for the door to open to him.

The post-chaise had brought him from Warwickshire, where, some six months before, he had been left an orphan. Now, owing to the generous offer of his elderly cousin, Mr Abney, he had come to live at Aswarby. The offer was unexpected, because all who knew anything of Mr Abney looked upon him as a somewhat austere recluse, into whose steady-going household the advent of a small boy would import a new and, it seemed, incongruous element. The truth is that very little was known of Mr Abney's pursuits or temper. The Professor of Greek at Cambridge had been heard to say that no one knew more of the religious beliefs of the later pagans than did the owner of Aswarby. Certainly his library contained all the then available books bearing on the Mysteries, the Orphic poems, the worship of Mithras, and the Neo-Platonists. In the marble-paved hall stood a fine group of Mithras slaying a bull, which had been imported from the Levant at great expense by the owner. He had contributed a description of it to the *Gentleman's Magazine*, and he had written a remarkable series of articles in the *Critical Museum* on the superstitions of the Romans of the Lower Empire. He was looked upon, in fine, as a man wrapped up in his books, and it was a matter of great surprise among his neighbours that he could even have heard of his orphan cousin, Stephen Elliott, much more that he should have volunteered to make him an inmate of Aswarby Hall.

Whatever may have been expected by his neighbours, it is certain that Mr Abney—the tall, the thin, the austere—seemed inclined to give his young cousin a kindly reception. The moment the front door was opened he darted out of his study, rubbing his hands with delight.

'How are you, my boy?—how are you? How old are you?' said he—'that is, you are not too much tired, I hope, by your journey to eat your supper?'

'No, thank you, sir,' said Master Elliott; 'I am pretty well.'

'That's a good lad,' said Mr Abney. 'And how old are you, my boy?'

It seemed a little odd that he should have asked the question twice in the first two minutes of their acquaintance.

'I'm twelve years old next birthday, sir,' said Stephen.

'And when is your birthday, my dear boy? Eleventh of September, eh? That's well—that's very well. Nearly a year hence, isn't it? I like—ha, ha!—I like to get these things down in my book. Sure it's twelve? Certain?'

'Yes, quite sure, sir.'

'Well, well! Take him to Mrs Bunch's room, Parkes, and let him have his tea—supper—whatever it is.'

'Yes, sir,' answered the staid Mr Parkes; and conducted Stephen to the lower regions.

Mrs Bunch was the most comfortable and human person whom Stephen had as yet met in Aswarby. She made him completely at home; they were great friends in a quarter of an hour: and great friends they remained. Mrs Bunch had been born in the neighbourhood some fifty-five years before the date of Stephen's arrival, and her residence at the Hall was of twenty years' standing. Consequently, if anyone knew the ins and outs of the house and the district, Mrs Bunch knew them; and she was by no means disinclined to communicate her information.

Certainly there were plenty of things about the Hall and the Hall gardens which Stephen, who was of an adventurous and inquiring turn, was anxious to have explained to him. 'Who built the temple at the end of the laurel walk? Who was the old man whose picture hung on the staircase, sitting at a table, with a skull under his hand?' These and many similar points were cleared up by the resources of Mrs Bunch's powerful intellect. There were others, however, of which the explanations furnished were less satisfactory.

One November evening Stephen was sitting by the fire in the housekeeper's room reflecting on his surroundings.

'Is Mr Abney a good man, and will he go to heaven?' he suddenly asked, with the peculiar confidence which children possess in the ability of their elders to settle these questions, the decision of which is believed to be reserved for other tribunals.

'Good?—bless the child!' said Mrs Bunch. 'Master's as kind a soul as ever I see! Didn't I never tell you of the little boy as he took in out of the street, as you may say, this seven years back? and the little girl, two years after I first come here?'

'No. Do tell me all about them, Mrs Bunch—now this minute!'

'Well,' said Mrs Bunch, 'the little girl I don't seem to recollect so much about. I know master brought her back with him from his walk one day, and give orders to Mrs Ellis, as was housekeeper then, as she should be took every care with. And the pore child hadn't no one belonging to her— she telled me so her own self—and here she lived with us a matter of three weeks it might be; and then, whether she were somethink of a gipsy in her blood or what not, but one morning she out of her bed afore any of us had opened an eye, and neither track nor yet trace of her have I set eyes on since. Master was wonderful put about, and had all the ponds dragged; but it's my belief she was had away by them gipsies, for there was singing round the house for as much as an hour the night she went, and Parkes, he declare as he heard them a-calling in the woods all that afternoon. Dear, dear! a hodd child she was, so silent in her ways and all, but I was wonderful taken up with her, so domesticated she was—surprising.'

'And what about the little boy?' said Stephen.

'Ah, that pore boy!' sighed Mrs Bunch. 'He were a foreigner—Jevanny he called hisself—and he come a-tweaking his 'urdy-gurdy round and about the drive one winter day, and master 'ad him in that minute, and ast all about where he came from, and how old he was, and how he made his way, and where was his relatives, and all as kind as heart could wish. But it went the same way with him. They're a hunruly lot, them foreign nations, I do suppose, and he was off one fine morning just the same as the girl. Why he went and what he done was our question for as much as a year after; for he never took his 'urdy-gurdy, and there it lays on the shelf.'

The remainder of the evening was spent by Stephen in miscellaneous cross-examination of Mrs Bunch and in efforts to extract a tune from the hurdy-gurdy.

That night he had a curious dream. At the end of the passage at the top of the house, in which his bedroom was situated, there was an old disused bathroom. It was kept locked, but the upper half of the door was glazed, and, since the muslin curtains which used to hang there had long been gone, you could look in and see the lead-lined bath affixed to the wall on the right hand, with its head towards the window.

On the night of which I am speaking, Stephen Elliott found himself, as he thought, looking through the glazed door. The moon was shining through the window, and he was gazing at a figure which lay in the bath.

His description of what he saw reminds me of what I once beheld myself in the famous vaults of St Michan's Church in Dublin, which possess the horrid property of preserving corpses from decay for centuries. A figure inexpressibly thin and pathetic, of a dusty leaden colour, enveloped in a shroud-like garment, the thin lips crooked into a faint and dreadful smile, the hands pressed tightly over the region of the heart.

As he looked upon it, a distant, almost inaudible moan seemed to issue from its lips, and the arms began to stir. The terror of the sight forced Stephen backwards, and he awake to the fact that he was indeed standing on the cold boarded floor of the passage in the full light of the moon. With a courage which I do not think can be common among boys of his age, he went to the door of the bathroom to ascertain if the figure of his dream were really there. It was not, and he went back to bed.

Mrs Bunch was much impressed next morning by his story, and went so far as to replace the muslin curtain over the glazed door of the bathroom. Mr Abney, moreover, to whom he confided his experiences at breakfast, was greatly interested, and made notes of the matter in what he called 'his book'.

The spring equinox was approaching, as Mr Abney frequently reminded his cousin, adding that this had been always considered by the ancients to be a critical time for the young: that Stephen would do well to take care of himself, and to shut his bedroom window at night; and that Censorinus had some valuable remarks on the subject. Two incidents that occurred about this time made an impression upon Stephen's mind.

The first was after an unusually uneasy and oppressed night that he had passed—though he could not recall any particular dream that he had had.

The following evening Mrs Bunch was occupying herself in mending his nightgown.

'Gracious me, Master Stephen!' she broke forth rather irritably, 'how do you manage to tear your nightdress all to flinders this way? Look here, sir, what trouble you do give to poor servants that have to darn and mend after you!'

There was indeed a most destructive and apparently wanton series of slits or scorings in the garment, which would undoubtedly require a skilful needle to make good. They were confined to the left side of the chest—long, parallel slits, about six inches in length, some of them not quite piercing the texture of the linen. Stephen could only express his entire ignorance of their origin: he was sure they were not there the night before.

'But,' he said, 'Mrs Bunch, they are just the same as the scratches on the outside of my bedroom door; and I'm sure I never had anything to do with making *them*.'

Mrs Bunch gazed at him open-mouthed, then snatched up a candle, departed hastily from the room, and was heard making her way upstairs. In a few minutes she came down.

'Well,' she said, 'Master Stephen, it's a funny thing to me how them marks and scratches can 'a' come there—too high up for any cat or dog to 'ave made 'em, much less a rat: for all the world like a Chinaman's finger-nails, as my uncle in the tea-trade used to tell us of when we was girls together. I wouldn't say nothing to master, not if I was you, Master Stephen, my dear; and just turn the key of the door when you go to your bed.'

'I always do, Mrs Bunch, as soon as I've said my prayers.'

'Ah, that's a good child: always say your prayers, and then no one can't hurt you.'

Herewith Mrs Bunch addressed herself to mending the injured nightgown, with intervals of meditation, until bedtime. This was on a Friday night in March, 1812.

On the following evening the usual duet of Stephen and Mrs Bunch was augmented by the sudden arrival of Mr Parkes, the butler, who as a rule kept himself rather *to* himself in his own pantry. He did not see that Stephen was there: he was, moreover, flustered, and less slow of speech than was his wont.

'Master may get up his own wine, if he likes, of an evening,' was his first remark. 'Either I do it in the daytime or not at all, Mrs Bunch. I don't know what it may be: very like it's the rats, or the wind got into the cellars; but I'm not so young as I was, and I can't go through with it as I have done.'

'Well, Mr Parkes, you know it is a surprising place for the rats, is the Hall.'

'I'm not denying that, Mrs Bunch; and, to be sure, many a time I've heard the tale from the men in the shipyards about the rat that could speak. I never laid no confidence in that before; but tonight, if I'd demeaned myself to lay my ear to the door of the further bin, I could pretty much have heard what they was saying.'

'Oh, there, Mr Parkes, I've no patience with your fancies! Rats talking in the wine-cellar indeed!'

'Well, Mrs Bunch, I've no wish to argue with you: all I say is, if you choose to go to the far bin, and lay your ear to the door, you may prove my words this minute.'

'What nonsense you do talk, Mr Parkes—not fit for children to listen to! Why, you'll be frightening Master Stephen there out of his wits.'

'What! Master Stephen?' said Parkes, awaking to the consciousness of the boy's presence. 'Master Stephen knows well enough when I'm a-playing a joke with you, Mrs Bunch.'

In fact, Master Stephen knew much too well to suppose that Parkes had in the first instance intended a joke. He was interested, not altogether pleasantly, in the situation; but all his questions were unsuccessful in inducing the butler to give any more detailed account of his experiences in the wine-cellar.

We have now arrived at March 24, 1812. It was a day of curious experiences for Stephen: a windy, noisy day, which filled the house and the gardens with a restless impression. As Stephen stood by the fence of the grounds, and looked out into the park, he felt as if an endless procession of unseen people were sweeping past him on the wind, borne on restlessly and aimlessly, vainly striving to stop themselves, to catch at something that might arrest their flight and bring them once again into contact with the living world of which they had formed a part. After luncheon that day Mr Abney said:

'Stephen, my boy, do you think you could manage to come

to me tonight as late as eleven o'clock in my study? I shall be busy until that time, and I wish to show you something connected with your future life which it is most important that you should know. You are not to mention this matter to Mrs Bunch nor to anyone else in the house; and you had better go to your room at the usual time.'

Here was a new excitement added to life: Stephen eagerly grasped at the opportunity of sitting up till eleven o'clock. He looked in at the library door on his way upstairs that evening, and saw a brazier, which he had often noticed in the corner of the room, moved out before the fire; an old silver-gilt cup stood on the table, filled with red wine, and some written sheets of paper lay near it. Mr Abney was sprinkling some incense on the brazier from a round silver box as Stephen passed, but did not seem to notice his step.

The wind had fallen, and there was a still night and a full moon. At about ten o'clock Stephen was standing at the open window of his bedroom, looking out over the country. Still as the night was, the mysterious population of the distant moonlit woods was not yet lulled to rest. From time to time strange cries as of lost and despairing wanderers sounded from across the mere. They might be the notes of owls or water-birds, yet they did not quite resemble either sound. Were not they coming nearer? Now they sounded from the nearer side of the water, and in a few moments they seemed to be floating about among the shrubberies. Then they ceased; but just as Stephen was thinking of shutting the window and resuming his reading of *Robinson Crusoe*, he caught sight of two figures standing on the gravelled terrace that ran along the garden side of the Hall—the figures of a boy and girl, as it seemed; they stood side by side, looking up at the windows. Something in the form of the girl recalled irresistibly his dream of the figure in the bath. The boy inspired him with more acute fear.

Whilst the girl stood still, half smiling, with her hands clasped over her heart, the boy, a thin shape, with black hair and ragged clothing, raised his arms in the air with an appearance of menace and of unappeasable hunger and longing. The moon shone upon his almost transparent hands, and Stephen saw that the nails were fearfully long and that the light shone through them. As he stood with his arms thus raised, he disclosed a terrifying spectacle. On the left side of his chest there opened a black and gaping rent; and there fell upon Stephen's brain, rather than upon his ear, the impression of one of those hungry and desolate cries that he had heard resounding over the woods of Aswarby all that evening. In another moment this dreadful pair had moved swiftly and noiselessly over the dry gravel, and he saw them no more.

Inexpressibly frightened as he was, he determined to take his candle and go down to Mr Abney's study, for the hour appointed for their meeting was near at hand. The study or library opened out of the front hall on one side, and Stephen, urged on by his terrors, did not take long in getting there. To effect an entrance was not so easy. The door was not locked, he felt sure, for the key was on the outside of it as usual. His repeated knocks produced no answer. Mr Abney was engaged: he was speaking. What! why did he try to cry out? and why was the cry choked in his throat? Had he, too, seen the mysterious children? But now everything was quiet, and the door yielded to Stephen's terrified and frantic pushing.

On the table in Mr Abney's study certain papers were found which explained the situation to Stephen Elliott when he was of an age to understand them. The most important sentences were as follows:

'It was a belief very strongly and generally held by the ancients—of whose wisdom in these matters I have had such experience as induces me to place confidence in their assertions—that by enacting certain processes which to us moderns have something of a barbaric complexion, a very remarkable enlightenment of the spiritual faculties in man may be attained: that, for example, by absorbing the personalities of a certain number of his fellow-creatures, an individual may gain a complete ascendancy over those orders of spiritual beings which control the elemental forces of our universe.

'It is recorded of Simon Magus that he was able to fly in the air, to become invisible, or to assume any form he pleased, by the agency of the soul of a boy whom, to use the libellous phrase employed by the author of the *Clementine Recognitions*, he had "murdered". I find it set down, moreover, with considerable detail in the writings of Hermes Trismegistus, that similar happy results may be produced by the absorption of the hearts of not less than three human beings below the age of twenty-one years. To the testing of the truth of this receipt I have devoted the greater part of the last twenty years, selecting as the *corpora vilia* of my experiment such persons as could conveniently be removed without occasioning a sensible gap in society. The first step I effected by the removal of one Phœbe Stanley, a girl of gipsy extraction, on March 24, 1792. The second, by the removal of a wandering Italian lad, named Giovanni Paoli, on the night of March 23, 1805. The final "victim"—to employ a word repugnant in the highest degree to my feelings—must be my cousin, Stephen Elliott. His day must be this March 24, 1812.

'The best means of effecting the required absorption is to remove the heart from the *living* subject, to reduce it to ashes, and to mingle them with about a pint of some red wine, preferably port. The remains of the first two subjects, at least, it will be well to conceal: a disused bathroom or winecellar will be found convenient for such a purpose. Some annoyance may be experienced from the psychic portion of the subjects, which popular language dignifies with the name of ghosts. But the man of philosophic temperament—to whom alone the experiment is appropriate—will be little prone to attach importance to the feeble efforts of these beings to wreak their vengeance on him. I contemplate with the liveliest satisfaction the enlarged and emancipated existence which the experiment, if successful, will confer on me; not only placing me beyond the reach of human justice (so-called), but eliminating to a great extent the prospect of death itself.'

Mr Abney was found in his chair, his head thrown back, his face stamped with an expression of rage, fright, and mortal pain. In his left side was a terrible lacerated wound, exposing the heart. There was no blood on his hands, and a long knife that lay on the table was perfectly clean. A savage wild-cat might have inflicted the injuries. The window of the study was open, and it was the opinion of the coroner that Mr Abney had met his death by the agency of some wild creature. But Stephen Elliott's study of the papers I have quoted led him to a very different conclusion.

The Doll's Ghost

FRANCIS MARION CRAWFORD

This next tale, "The Doll's Ghost", is a rather different kind of spook story, for the apparition here is not human—if it is fair to say that any of them are human, that is! It is also an evocative story of the early years of the twentieth century when our towns were full of big houses, horse-drawn carriages clip-clopping through the evening streets and gas lamps throwing flickering, eerie shadows across the pavements. Far more frightening to think of being lost then in such a situation than in our modern cities with their apartment blocks, wide streets and bright neon lighting, isn't it? In any event, that is what "The Doll's Ghost" is all about, and the part played by a toy in the search for a missing child. The author, Francis Marion Crawford, was an American and enjoyed much the same popularity on that side of the Atlantic as a teller of frightening stories as Professor James did in Britain. But he also knew and loved London as he clearly shows in this unusual and certainly uncanny story.

It was a terrible accident, and for one moment the splendid machinery of Cranston House got out of gear and stood still. The butler emerged from the retirement in which he spent his elegant leisure, two grooms of the chambers appeared simultaneously from opposite directions, there were actually housemaids on the grand staircase, and those who remember the facts most exactly assert that Mrs Pringle herself positively stood upon the landing. Mrs Pringle was the housekeeper. As for the head nurse, the under nurse, and the nursery-maid, their feelings cannot be described. The head nurse laid one hand upon the polished marble balustrade and stared stupidly before her, the under nurse stood rigid and pale, leaning against the polished marble wall, and the nursery-maid collapsed and sat down upon the polished marble step, just beyond the limits of the velvet carpet, and frankly burst into tears.

The Lady Gwendolen Lancaster-Douglas-Scroop, youngest daughter of the ninth Duke of Cranston, and aged six years and three months, picked herself up quite alone, and sat down on the third step from the foot of the grand staircase in Cranston House.

'Oh!' ejaculated the butler, and he disappeared again.

'Ah!' responded the grooms of the chambers, as they also went away.

'It's only that doll,' Mrs Pringle was distinctly heard to say, in a tone of contempt.

The under nurse heard her say it. Then the three nurses gathered round Lady Gwendolen and patted her, and gave her unhealthy things out of their pockets, and hurried her out of Cranston House as fast as they could, lest it should be found out upstairs that they had allowed the Lady Gwendolen Lancaster-Douglas-Scroop to tumble down the grand staircase with her doll in her arms. And as the doll was badly broken, the nursery-maid carried it, with the pieces, wrapped up in Lady Gwendolen's little cloak. It was not far to Hyde Park, and when they had reached a quiet place they took means to find out that Lady Gwendolen had no bruises. For the carpet was very thick and soft, and there was thick stuff under it to make it softer.

Lady Gwendolen Douglas-Scroop sometimes yelled, but she never cried. It was because she had yelled that the nurse had allowed her to go downstairs alone with Nina, the doll, under one arm, while she steadied herself with her other hand on the balustrade, and trod upon the polished marble steps beyond the edge of the carpet. So she had fallen, and Nina had come to grief.

When the nurses were quite sure that she was not hurt, they unwrapped the doll and looked at her in her turn. She had been a very beautiful doll, very large, and fair, and healthy, with real yellow hair, and eyelids that would open and shut over very grown-up dark eyes. Moreover, when you moved her right arm up and down she said 'Pa-pa,' and when you moved the left she said 'Ma-ma' very distinctly.

'I heard her say "Pa" when she fell,' said the under nurse, who heard everything. 'But she ought to have said "Pa-pa".'

'That's because her arm went up when she hit the step,' said the head nurse. 'She'll say the other "Pa" when I put it down again.'

'Pa,' said Nina, as her right arm was pushed down, and speaking through her broken face. It was cracked right across, from the upper corner of the forehead, with a hideous gash, through the nose and down to the little frilled collar of the pale green silk Mother Hubbard frock, and two little three-cornered pieces of porcelain had fallen out.

'I'm sure it's a wonder she can speak at all, being all smashed,' said the under nurse.

'You'll have to take her to Mr Puckler,' said her superior. 'It's not far, and you'd better go at once.'

Lady Gwendolen was occupied in digging a hole in the ground with a little spade, and paid no attention to the nurses.

'What are you doing?' inquired the nursery-maid, looking on.

'Nina's dead, and I'm diggin' her a grave,' replied her ladyship thoughtfully.

'Oh, she'll come to life again all right,' said the nursery-maid.

The under nurse wrapped Nina up again and departed. Fortunately a kind soldier, with very long legs and a very small cap, happened to be there; and as he had nothing to do, he offered to see the under nurse safely to Mr Puckler's and back.

Mr Bernard Puckler and his little daughter lived in a little house in a little alley, which led out of a quiet little street not very far from Belgrave Square. He was the great doll doctor, and his extensive practice lay in the most aristocratic quarter. He mended dolls of all sizes and ages, boy dolls and girl dolls, baby dolls in long clothes, and grown-up dolls in fashionable gowns, talking dolls and dumb dolls, those that shut their eyes when they lay down, and those whose eyes had to be shut for them by means of a mysterious wire. His daughter Else was only just over twelve years old, but she was already very clever at mending dolls' clothes, and at doing their hair, which is harder than you might think, though the dolls sit quite still while it is being done.

Mr Puckler had originally been a German, but he had dissolved his nationality in the ocean of London many years ago, like a great many foreigners. He still had one or two German friends, however, who came on Saturday evenings, and smoked with him and played picquet or 'skat' with him for farthing points, and called him 'Herr Doctor', which seemed to please Mr Puckler very much.

He looked older than he was, for his beard was rather long and ragged, his hair was grizzled and thin, and he wore horn-rimmed spectacles. As for Else, she was a thin, pale child, very quiet and neat, with dark eyes and brown hair that was plaited down her back and tied with a bit of black ribbon. She mended the dolls' clothes and took the dolls back to their homes when they were quite strong again.

The house was a little one, but too big for the two people who lived in it. There was a small sitting-room on the street, and the workshop was at the back, and there were three rooms upstairs. But the father and daughter lived most of their time in the workshop, because they were generally at work, even in the evenings.

Mr Puckler laid Nina on the table and looked at her a long time, till the tears began to fill his eyes behind the horn-rimmed spectacles. He was a very susceptible man, and he often fell in love with the dolls he mended, and found it hard to part with them when they had smiled at him for a few days. They were real little people to him, with characters and thoughts and feelings of their own, and he was very tender with them all. But some attracted him especially from the first, and when they were brought to him maimed and injured, their state seemed so pitiful to him that the tears came easily. You must remember that he had lived among dolls during a great part of his life, and understood them.

'How do you know that they feel nothing?' he went on to say to Else. 'You must be gentle with them. It costs nothing to be kind to the little beings, and perhaps it makes a difference to them.'

And Else understood him, because she was a child, and she knew that she was more to him than all the dolls.

He fell in love with Nina at first sight, perhaps because her beautiful brown glass eyes were something like Else's own, and he loved Else first and best, with all his heart. And, besides, it was a very sorrowful case. Nina had evidently not been long in the world, for her complexion was perfect, her hair was smooth where it should be smooth, and curly where it should be curly, and her silk clothes were perfectly new. But across her face was that frightful gash, like a sabre-cut, deep and shadowy within, but clean and sharp at the edges. When he tenderly pressed her head to close the gaping wound, the edges made a fine grating sound, that was painful to hear, and the lids of the dark eyes quivered and trembled as though Nina were suffering dreadfully.

'Poor Nina!' he exclaimed sorrowfully. 'But I shall not hurt you much, though you will take a long time to get strong.'

He always asked the names of the broken dolls when they were brought to him, and sometimes the people knew what the children called them, and told him. He liked 'Nina' for a name. Altogether and in every way she pleased him more than any doll he had seen for many years, and he felt drawn to her, and made up his mind to make her perfectly strong and sound, no matter how much labour it might cost him.

Mr Puckler worked patiently a little at a time, and Else watched him. She could do nothing for poor Nina, whose clothes needed no mending. The longer the doll doctor worked, the more fond he became of the yellow hair and the beautiful brown glass eyes. He sometimes forgot all the other dolls that were waiting to be mended, lying side by side on a shelf, and sat for an hour gazing at Nina's face, while he racked his ingenuity for some new invention by which to hide even the smallest trace of the terrible accident.

She was wonderfully mended. Even he was obliged to admit that; but the scar was still visible to his keen eyes, a very fine line right across the face, downwards from right to left. Yet all the conditions had been most favourable for a cure, since the cement had set quite hard at the first attempt and the weather had been fine and dry, which makes a great difference in a dolls' hospital.

At last he knew that he could do no more, and the under nurse had already come twice to see whether the job was finished, as she coarsely expressed it.

'Nina is not quite strong yet,' Mr Puckler had answered each time, for he could not make up his mind to face the parting.

And now he sat before the square deal table at which he worked, and Nina lay before him for the last time with a big brown-paper box beside her. It stood there like her coffin, waiting for her, he thought. He must put her into it, and lay tissue-paper over her dear face, and then put on the lid, and at the thought of tying the string his sight was dim with tears again. He was never to look into the glassy depths of the beautiful brown eyes any more, nor to hear the little wooden voice say 'Pa-pa' and 'Ma-ma'. It was a very painful moment.

In the vain hope of gaining time before the separation, he took up the little sticky bottles of cement and glue and gum and colour, looking at each one in turn, and then at Nina's face. And all his small tools lay there, neatly arranged in a row, but he knew that he could not use them again for Nina. She was quite strong at last, and in a country where there should be no cruel children to hurt her she might live a hundred years, with only that almost imperceptible line across her face, to tell of the fearful thing that had befallen her on the marble steps of Cranston House.

Suddenly Mr Puckler's heart was quite full, and he rose abruptly from his seat and turned away.

'Else,' he said unsteadily, 'you must do it for me. I cannot bear to see her go into the box.'

So he went and stood at the window with his back turned, while Else did what he had not the heart to do.

'Is it done?' he asked, not turning round. 'Then take her away, my dear. Put on your hat, and take her to Cranston House quickly, and when you are gone I will turn round.'

Else was used to her father's queer ways with the dolls, and though she had never seen him so much moved by a parting, she was not much surprised.

'Come back quickly,' he said, when he heard her hand on the latch. 'It is growing late, and I should not send you at this hour. But I cannot bear to look forward to it any more.'

When Else was gone, he left the window and sat down in his place before the table again, to wait for the child to come back. He touched the place where Nina had lain, very gently, and he recalled the softly-tinted pink face, and the glass eyes, and the ringlets of yellow hair, till he could almost see them.

The evenings were long, for it was late in the spring. But it began to grow dark soon, and Mr Puckler wondered why Else did not come back. She had been gone an hour and a half, and that was much longer than he had expected, for it was barely half a mile from Belgrave Square to Cranston House. He reflected that the child might have been kept waiting, but as the twilight deepened he grew anxious, and walking up and down in the dim workshop, no longer thinking of Nina, but of Else, his own living child, whom he loved.

An undefinable, disquieting sensation came upon him by fine degrees, a chilliness and a faint stirring of his thin hair, joined with a wish to be in any company rather than to be alone much longer. It was the beginning of fear.

He told himself in strong German-English that he was a

foolish old man, and he began to feel about for the matches in the dusk. He knew just where they should be, for he always kept them in the same place, close to the little tin box that held bits of sealing-wax of various colours, for some kinds of mending. But somehow he could not find the matches in the gloom.

Something had happened to Else, he was sure, and as his fear increased, he felt as though it might be allayed if he could get a light and see what time it was. Then he called himself a foolish old man again, and the sound of his own voice startled him in the dark. He could not find the matches.

The window was grey still; he might see what time it was if he went close to it, and he could go and get matches out of the cupboard afterwards. He stood back from the table, to get out of the way of the chair, and began to cross the board floor.

Something was following him in the dark. There was a small pattering, as of tiny feet upon the boards. He stopped and listened, and the roots of his hair tingled. It was nothing, and he was a foolish old man. He made two steps more, and he was sure that he heard the little pattering again. He turned his back to the window, leaning against the sash so that the panes began to crack, and he faced the dark. Everything was quite still, and it smelt of paste and cement and wood-filings as usual.

'Is that you, Else?' he asked, and he was surprised by the fear in his voice.

There was no answer in the room, and he held up his watch and tried to make out what time it was by the grey dusk that was just not darkness. So far as he could see, it was within two or three minutes of ten o'clock. He had been a long time alone. He was shocked, and frightened for Else, out in London, so late, and he almost ran across the room to the door. As he fumbled for the latch, he distinctly heard the running of the little feet after him.

'Mice!' he exclaimed feebly, just as he got the door open. He shut it quickly behind him, and felt as though some cold thing had settled on his back and were writhing upon him. The passage was quite dark, but he found his hat and was out in the alley in a moment, breathing more freely, and surprised to find how much light there still was in the open air. He could see the pavement clearly under his feet, and far off in the street to which the alley led he could hear the laughter and calls of children, playing some game out of doors. He wondered how he could have been so nervous, and for an instant he thought of going back into the house to wait quietly for Else. But instantly he felt that nervous fright of something stealing over him again. In any case it was better to walk up to Cranston House and ask the servants about the child. One of the women had perhaps taken a fancy to her, and was even now giving her tea and cake.

He walked quickly to Belgrave Square, and then up the broad streets, listening as he went, whenever there was no other sound, for the tiny footsteps. But he heard nothing, and was laughing at himself when he rang the servants' bell at the big house. Of course, the child must be there.

The person who opened the door was quite an inferior person, for it was a back-door, but affected the manners of the front, and stared at Mr Puckler superciliously under the strong light.

No little girl had been seen, and he knew 'nothing about no dolls'.

'She is my little girl,' said Mr Puckler tremulously, for all his anxiety was returning tenfold, 'and I am afraid something has happened.'

The inferior person said rudely that 'nothing could have happened to her in that house, because she had not been there, which was a jolly good reason why'; and Mr Puckler was obliged to admit that the man ought to know, as it was his business to keep the door and let people in. He wished to be allowed to speak to the under nurse, who knew him; but the man was ruder than ever, and finally shut the door in his face.

When the doll doctor was alone in the street, he steadied

himself by the railing, for he felt as though he was breaking in two, just as some dolls break, in the middle of the backbone.

Presently he knew that he must be doing something to find Else, and that gave him strength. He began to walk as quickly as he could through the streets, following every highway and byway which his little girl might have taken on her errand. He also asked several policemen in vain if they had seen her, and most of them answered him kindly, for they saw that he was a sober man and in his right senses, and some of them had little girls of their own.

It was one o'clock in the morning when he went up to his own door again, worn out and hopeless and broken-hearted. As he turned the key in the lock, his heart stood still, for he knew that he was awake and not dreaming, and that he really heard those tiny footsteps pattering to meet him inside the house along the passage.

But he was too unhappy to be much frightened any more, and his heart went on again with a dull regular pain, that found its way all through him with every pulse. So he went in, and hung up his hat in the dark, and found the matches in the cupboard and the candlestick in its place in the corner.

Mr Puckler was so much overcome and so completely worn out that he sat down in his chair before the worktable and almost fainted, as his face dropped forward upon his folded hands. Beside him the solitary candle burned steadily with a low flame in the still warm air.

'Else! Else!' he moaned against his yellow knuckles. And that was all he could say, and it was no relief to him. On the contrary, the very sound of the name was a new and sharp pain that pierced his ears and his head and his very soul. For every time he repeated the name it meant that little Else was dead, somewhere out in the streets of London in the dark.

He was so terribly hurt that he did not even feel something pulling gently at the skirt of his old coat, so gently that it was like the nibbling of a tiny mouse. He might have thought that it was really a mouse if he had noticed it.

'Else! Else!' he groaned, right against his hands.

Then a cool breath stirred his thin hair, and the low flame of the one candle dropped down almost to a mere spark, not flickering as though a draught were going to blow it out, but just dropping down as if it were tired out. Mr Puckler felt his hands stiffening with fright under his face; and there was a faint rustling sound, like some small silk thing blown in a gentle breeze. He sat up straight, stark and scared, and a small wooden voice spoke in the stillness.

'Pa-pa,' it said, with a break between the syllables.

Mr Puckler stood up in a single jump, and his chair fell over backwards with a smashing noise upon the wooden floor. The candle had almost gone out.

It was Nina's doll-voice that had spoken, and he should have known it among the voices of a hundred other dolls. And yet there was something more in it, a little human ring, with a pitiful cry and a call for help, and the wail of a hurt child. Mr Puckler stood up, stark and stiff, and tried to look round, but at first he could not, for he seemed to be frozen from head to foot.

Then he made a great effort, and he raised one hand to each of his temples, and pressed his own head round as he would have turned a doll's. The candle was burning so low that it might as well have been out altogether, for any light it gave, and the room seemed quite dark at first. Then he saw something. He would not have believed that he could be more frightened than he had been just before that. But he was, and his knees shook, for he saw the doll standing in the middle of the floor, shining with a faint and ghostly radiance, her beautiful glassy brown eyes fixed on his. And across her face the very thin line of the break he had mended shone as though it were drawn in light with a fine point of white flame.

Yet there was something more in the eyes, too; there was something human, like Else's own, but as if only the doll saw him through them, and not Else. And there was enough of Else to bring back all his pain and to make him forget his fear.

'Else! My little Else!' he cried aloud.

The small ghost moved, and its doll-arm slowly rose and fell with a stiff, mechanical motion.

'Pa-pa,' it said.

It seemed this time that there was even more of Else's tone echoing somewhere between the wooden notes that reached his ears so distinctly, and yet so far away. Else was calling him, he was sure.

His face was perfectly white in the gloom, but his knees did not shake any more, and he felt that he was less frightened.

'Yes, child! But where? Where?' he asked. 'Where are you, Else?'

'Pa-pa!'

The syllables died away in the quiet room. There was a low rustling of silk, the glassy brown eyes turned slowly away, and Mr Puckler heard the pitter-patter of the small feet in the bronze kid slippers as the figure ran straight to the door. Then the candle burned high again, the room was full of light, and he was alone.

Mr Puckler passed his hand over his eyes and looked about him. He could see everything quite clearly, and he felt that he must have been dreaming, though he was standing instead of sitting down, as he should have been if he had just waked up. The candle burned brightly now. There were the dolls to be mended, lying in a row with their toes up. The third one had lost her right shoe, and Else was making one. He knew that, and he was certainly not dreaming now. He had not been dreaming when he had come in from his fruitless search and had heard the doll's footsteps running to the door. He had not fallen asleep in his chair. How could he possibly have fallen asleep when his heart was breaking? He had been awake all the time.

He steadied himself, set the fallen chair upon its legs, and said to himself again very emphatically that he was a foolish old man. He ought to be out in the streets looking for his child, asking questions, and inquiring at the police-stations, where all accidents were reported as soon as they were known, or at the hospitals.

'Pa-pa!'

The longing, wailing, pitiful little wooden cry rang from the passage, outside the door, and Mr Puckler stood for an instant with white face, transfixed and rooted to the spot. A moment later his hand was on the latch. Then he was in the passage, with the light streaming from the open door behind him.

Quite at the other end he saw the little phantom shining clearly in the shadow, and the right hand seemed to beckon to him as the arm rose and fell once more. He knew all at once that it had not come to frighten him but to lead him, and when it disappeared, and he walked boldly towards the door, he knew that it was in the street outside, waiting for him. He forgot that he was tired and had eaten no supper, and had walked many miles, for a sudden hope ran through and through him, like a golden stream of life.

And sure enough, at the corner of the alley, and at the corner of the street, and out in Belgrave Square, he saw the small ghost flitting before him. Sometimes it was only a shadow, where there was other light, but then the glare of the lamps made a pale green sheen on its little Mother Hubbard frock of silk; and sometimes, where the streets were dark and silent, the whole figure shone out brightly, with its yellow curls and rosy neck. It seemed to trot along like a tiny child, and Mr Puckler could almost hear the pattering of the bronze kid slippers on the pavement as it ran. But it went very fast, and he could only just keep up with it, tearing along with his hat on the back of his head and his thin hair blown by the night breeze, and his horn-rimmed spectacles firmly set upon his broad nose.

On and on he went, and he had no idea where he was. He did not even care, for he knew certainly that he was going the right way.

Then at last, in a wide, quiet street, he was standing before a big, sober-looking door that had two lamps on each side of it, and a polished brass bell-handle, which he pulled.

And just inside, when the door was opened, in the bright light, there was the little shadow, and the pale green sheen of the little silk dress, and once more the small cry came to his ears, less pitiful, more longing.

'Pa-pa!'

The shadow turned suddenly bright, and out of the brightness the beautiful brown glass eyes were turned up happily to his, while the rosy mouth smiled so divinely that the phantom doll looked almost like a little angel just then.

'A little girl was brought in soon after ten o'clock,' said the quiet voice of the hospital doorkeeper. 'I think they thought she was only stunned. She was holding a big brown-paper box against her, and they could not get it out of her arms. She had a long plait of brown hair that hung down as they carried her.'

'She is my little girl,' said Mr Puckler, but he hardly heard his own voice.

He leaned over Else's face in the gentle light of the children's ward, and when he had stood there a minute the beautiful brown eyes opened and looked up to his.

'Pa-pa!' cried Else softly, 'I knew you would come!'

Then Mr Puckler did not know what he did or said for a moment, and what he felt was worth all the fear and terror and despair that had almost killed him that night. But by-and-by Else was telling her story, and the nurse let her speak, for there were only two other children in the room, who were getting well and were sound asleep.

'They were big boys with bad faces,' said Else, 'and they tried to get Nina away from me, but I held on and fought as well as I could till one of them hit me with something, and I don't remember any more, for I tumbled down, and I suppose the boys ran away, and somebody found me there. But I'm afraid Nina is all smashed.'

'Here is the box,' said the nurse. 'We could not take it out of her arms till she came to herself. Should you like to see if the doll is broken?'

And she undid the string cleverly, but Nina was all smashed to pieces. Only the gentle light of the children's ward made a pale green sheen in the folds of the little Mother Hubbard frock.

Nurse's Tale

H. R. WAKEFIELD

As I indicated in the introduction, I heard my first tale of terror as a youngster at the knee of an old relative and I am sure this is how many of us get our earliest taste of the unknown. In the following story, a small boy with an obvious delight in such things is told a rather special tale by his Nanny; and although Nannies and nurseries are no longer so commonplace as they used to be, I think it is quite fair to say that this account could just as easily be told by a parent or relative in an ordinary bedroom. The story is all about a terrible curse which has been laid on a noble family, and although written fifty years ago it is still fresh and exciting. The author, H. R. Wakefield, is another outstanding writer of supernatural stories, and in one of my earlier collections (The Ghost's Companion) *I included a story by him based on his own experiences in a haunted house. There are some elements of a tale he heard as a child in "Nurse's Story", and I am sure the fate of young Master Jocelyn will give you more than a little cause to shudder!*

'Thanks awfully, Nurse; it's just what I wanted. But now I'm ten you've got to tell me about that kid Layton. You promised you would.'

'I don't believe I ever promised.'

'Yes, you did, you old fiend.'

'You mustn't use such expressions, Master Gilbert, they're rude! You're too old for your age, that's what you are! And you read too many of those ghost books. That James, he gives me the creeps!'

'Oh, I love them, Nurse; especially, *Oh, whistle and I'll come to you!*'

'That one about the bedclothes getting up and walking about, just when they'd made the bed, too? I can't see why people want to think of such things.'

'Well, I'm ten and you promised.'

'And I hope you'll behave like ten; it's time you did. I dare say the other Marlborough boys will take you down a peg or two, when you get there.'

'I shan't funk them. And shut up, Nurse, and shoot the works!'

'Wherever did you learn that vulgar saying?'

'At the cinema. Oh, go on!'

'And give you dreams and get into trouble with your mamma. You're such a pest! Well, I'll tell you, but don't blame me if you can't sleep. Anyway, I know I shan't have any peace till I *do* tell you. Now, sit still and don't shuffle about.

'It's about twenty-five years since I first went to Layton Hall. Lady Layton died the night I arrived, poor dear, and the funeral and the christening took place within a few days of each other. His Lordship was terribly sad. He was a fine gentleman, every inch a lord. He was very tall, and handsome and quiet, and at first he didn't seem to take to the baby—Jocelyn they named him—but then afterwards he could hardly keep his thoughts off him. At first I wondered why he seemed so watchful and anxious, but one day the head gardener told me there was a sort of mystery about the family. The story was that a long while ago—hundreds of years—they burnt a witch, at least I think she was a witch—some bad lot, anyway—'

'But, Nurse, you don't believe in witches, do you?'

'I don't believe either way, but where I was brought up plenty did. But, as I say, they burnt one of them, and her small boy too. And it seems he was near his sixth birthday, and this witch put a curse on the family—that was the talk, anyway—saying that no Layton's eldest son would live to be six. And they never had done after that. So the place was always going to different parts of the family. And that was why his Lordship was so anxious about Master Jocelyn. He was a beautiful baby, and very good—too good, I used to think. For he hardly ever cried, not even when he was cutting his teeth, and healthy babies ought to cry. You used to cry till I could have choked you, you young limb, but then you were never good. Now, don't pinch or I won't tell you any more. Not that he was sickly, but he seemed to be thinking his own thoughts all the while. But the first time I found something really funny about him was when he was about nine months old. At Layton there is a long drive from the road to the Hall, twisting and hilly, and about half-way up there was a dip in it—a sort of valley. It was a lovely quiet spot, cut off from everything, with fields on either side. It always used to give me the creeps a bit; I mean I wouldn't have walked along there alone after dark if I could have helped it.'

'I wouldn't have minded. I bet I'd have gone!'

'Oh, you're very brave and full of swank in the morning with people about. But you weren't so brave in the cloisters at Norwich!'

'Well, something began to tap on the other side of the big door just as I reached it; and I thought it was beginning to open. And there wasn't anyone in the Cathedral. Anyway, I was partly pretending.'

'Did you put chalk on your face? That was white enough. Now, don't keep on interrupting. Well, as I said, it was just about Master Jocelyn's ninth month that I found he was queer about that bit of drive. As we got near it he'd waken and sit up in his pram and keep his eyes fixed on the field on the left side—coming down, that is. And he wouldn't lie down until we began to go up the hill on the other side, however much I tried to make him. And then the pucker left his little forehead and he'd lie back and go to sleep again. As he got older he seemed to get more and more interested in that bit of the drive, and when he learned to walk he always insisted on getting out and going into the field, and almost the first thing he ever said after he'd learned to talk was, "Pitty tees," when he was out on the grass.'

'But I thought you said it was just a field?'

'So it was. There was a tree or two, but they was on the other side of the drive.'

'Then—'

'Now, Master Gilbert, don't keep on stopping me in the middle. I'm just telling you what happened. And what happened was that Master Jocelyn always behaved as if there was trees. It used to worry me—it wasn't natural—and I tried to get him past that dip, but he wouldn't let me, and then I tried keeping him in the garden, but he wouldn't let me do that either, but cried and made a fuss till I took him down the drive again. And it wasn't so much that he seemed happy in the field as anxious to be there. And there was he in a wood all the time and me in a field. It seemed to me I ought to mention it to his Lordship. So I did, and for a moment he looked away from me, as if he was upset and not sure what to say. And then he said, "Have you tried to keep him away from there?" And I said I had but that it wasn't any use. And he said, "Well, then—" and he paused for a bit. "Well, then, let him play there, but don't let him wander off by himself." I was sorry I'd told him in a way, but I thought I ought to.'

'What was the field like? Were there stumps of trees there? Had it been a wood?'

'No, it was just an ordinary grass field.'

'Did you see any birds or animals in it?'

'No; why do you ask that?'

'I don't know exactly.'

'Well, it's a fact I never saw bird or beast in that field except a dead rabbit once. The gardener picked it up and had a look at it, but he couldn't find anything wrong with it, so he said it must have died of old age, and he threw it away. Master Jocelyn was always drawing pictures of a wood, and he was clever at it and made it look real. But he always drew the same one with a big tree in the middle. But he couldn't seem to draw the big tree properly, but always made a red and black smudge around it. And it was a funny thing how he always made straight for the place where that big tree would have been if there had been a wood, and then he'd look up. And he used to pick his way along as if he was dodging trees, and following some sort of pathway. He talked very little and always seemed to be thinking his own thoughts. He grew up into the most lovely little boy. He learnt his lessons all right, but not as if he cared so much about them, though he was very quick and sharp about some things.'

'When he was in the field, could he see you?'

'What questions you ask! Well, I can't be sure; he never looked at me or said a word. He just wandered about, and I got out of the way of speaking to him, though I always kept an eye on him.'

'Did it put the wind up you?'

'There you are with your vulgar talk! I always felt a bit uneasy, but I got used to it and didn't bother as a rule. But sometimes when I got drowsy and day-dreaming I'd think for a second or two I *was* in a wood and hearing a sort of rustle of leaves, and get a feeling that someone was watching me; but then I'd come to myself and know I'd been imagining things. We lived a very quiet life, with just a break of six weeks every summer when we went to Bognor—the doctor said the air there was good for Master Jocelyn. He seemed to like the seaside, though I couldn't get him to make friends with other children. But he liked his bathe and sitting on the beach and watching the water. And he loved the boats.'

'You don't see any decent liners at Bognor, only dull old tramps. Deal's the place.'

'Oh, well, he wasn't so particular, nor such a Johnny-Know-all as you. But I believe he was nearly always thinking of the wood. He used to try and draw it on the sand with a shell.

'Things went on much the same till just after his fifth birthday, and then I felt more bothered about him, for I got the idea that he was seeing someone in the field.'

'Why did you think that, Nurse?'

'Now, wasn't I just going to tell you, impatient? Well,

mostly from the way he stared and looked about him. He seemed to be following something around—watching it. And as he didn't look up or down I took it that it was something or someone about his own size. I asked him what it was, though I never liked to put questions about the field. He didn't answer, but looked away from me. I felt it was a sort of secret of his and that I was left out of it.

'His Lordship asked me now and again how I found him, and I had to say he was a queer little chap, though as good as gold. I still love him, the sweet angel!'

'Better than me?'

'Well, you're not so bad, Master Gilbert, when you try to behave, which isn't often. Now, stop rubbing your toes together, those shoes have got to last you.

'I could see the master knew what I meant when I said, "queer". He looked as if there was nothing to be done. He used to spend an hour or two a day with Master Jocelyn, but I don't believe they was quite easy together. The little boy was fond of him and liked sitting on his knee or lying back against his shoulder, but it was always the same story, he thought his own thoughts, and neither his father nor me came into them much of the time. And I think his Lordship knew that and felt badly about it; and I used to get the idea that he'd given up hope, though he'd hardly confess it to himself. Layton seemed to make him worried and he used to spend a lot of time in London. He looked ill and tired and restless. But when Master Jocelyn's sixth birthday came near he stayed in the house, and, of course, I knew why. I kept the little boy near me night and day—it made me dream and sleep badly, for I had a feeling that the trouble was coming.'

'What sort of trouble?'

'Well, haven't I told you about the curse and what always happened?'

'Yes, but—'

'Now, then, you're interrupting again. I just felt that I'd got to see that Master Jocelyn had someone on his side and fighting for him and that it wouldn't be my fault if the curse worked again. As the birthday drew near, his Lordship was like a cat on hot bricks, and I could have screamed sometimes, my nerves were so on edge. His birthday was on March 21st. During the week before we'd been in the field every day and I'd watched him like a knife. March 20th was a very wild and windy day and Master Jocelyn seemed restless and broody, but all the same, when we went out in the afternoon I felt the worst was over, for what could happen between then and midnight? It was very dark for that time of year. Now, I don't know how to explain it, but as soon as we'd gone into the field everything seemed strange, as if it *was* a wood, and I thought I heard the trees fighting with the wind, and for a bit I forgot Master Jocelyn, and I think I sat down and felt silly—as if I was someone else. And then suddenly I heard a shout and came to myself, and I couldn't see Master Jocelyn. So I started to run, and I remember twisting and dodging as if I was running through a wood, and I turned a corner, and there was Master Jocelyn lying on his face, just about where that big tree would have been. When I reached him it was just a field again and he stretched out on the grass. He was in a faint. I ran with him in my arms back to the house. As I got near, his Lordship came dashing out to meet me, and he took him from me without a word. I was so out of breath that I had to lie down on the lawn, and I thought my heart would burst. As soon as I could manage it, I got to the house. His Lordship was giving Master Jocelyn brandy in his study and the footman was rushing off on his bicycle for the doctor. And then his Lordship carried Master Jocelyn up to my bedroom, where he slept. He was dead white and his eyes was shut, but he couldn't keep still. He kept twisting and throwing out his arms, and then he began to mutter—on and on and on—and presently he'd scream. When the doctor came he asked me what had happened, and I told him, but he never looked at the master. And then he pulled up Master Jocelyn's sleeves, and I could see his little arms was burnt past the elbow. And the doctor said nothing, but got me to fetch bandages and vaseline, and we did all we could for the little boy. But nothing we did was any good. He kept twisting and shifting and throwing out his arms and always gave that scream. The doctor said he wasn't really in pain, for he was quite unconscious. Just before twelve o'clock he cried out, "Mummie!" very loud three times—and died.

'I can still remember how the wind was roaring, and how when he cried out the wind seemed to catch his cry and carry it far, far away.

'They buried him three days later. The master kept himself shut up in his room all the time. The family had a vault in Layton Church, and the coffin was taken to it in a farm cart. The wind had gone by then and it was a queer, dark, close afternoon, not a bit like any March day I've ever seen. I remember I walked behind the cart with the master, though otherwise I've always been a bit hazy about that day. We had to go down the drive, for the church was just off the main road. Well, just as we reached the middle of that field something seemed to flash down from the sky and there was a great flame before my eyes. And I seemed to see Master Jocelyn jump down from the cart and start to run along the path through the wood. And I went after him. And it *was* a wood this time, and very dark. But ahead I could see a big red glare and, as I got near flames above it. And they came from the same spot by the big tree. And all the time I could see Master Jocelyn running ahead of me. And then I turned a corner, and there was a great pile of flaming wood and I could hear it roaring. And I seemed to be running through a big crowd of people who made way for me. And Master Jocelyn ran straight into the fire and disappeared. Then, just as I reached the blaze I heard him scream and I saw his little arms flung above the flames. And I tried to reach up to him, but the flames came out at me—and the next thing I knew was waking up at the Klerkley Cottage Hospital and finding my arms all bandaged up and most of the hair burnt off my head. I didn't understand what had happened for a day or two because they wouldn't let me talk. But when I was better they told me I'd been struck by lightning and knocked down silly for three days, and that was really how I got the burns.'

'But what happened to Lord Layton if he was walking beside you?'

'Now, don't you worry about that, because I'm not going to tell you. And I suppose you'll have dreams and I'll get the blame. But you pester so and you're always reading those horrid ghost books.'

'But tell me, Nurse, why—'

'I shan't tell you another word. You get on with that drawing of the house while I wake Miss Dolly and take her some Benger's. And don't kick your toes together. Those shoes have got to last.'

The Attic

ALGERNON BLACKWOOD

As a slightly older child, I remember that one of the highlights of my week was to be allowed to stay up late and listen to Algernon Blackwood reading his stories of terror and mystery on the radio. There was something about his voice and the atmosphere that he managed to get into these tales that made your hair curl and your mind imagine far more frightening things than any film or television programme could show you. He based these stories on all sorts of strange things that had happened to him during a life-time of travelling around the world and exploring mysterious, out-of-the-way places. I particularly remember his experience on a haunted island in Canada, and the horrifying slithering sound that drove him nearly mad in an American boarding house. Lots of his stories take place at night, and it has not been easy selecting one for this collection. Finally, though, I have settled for "The Attic" because most of us have one in our homes and it is not difficult to imagine the strangest things happening there. And also because I can still hear the author's sombre voice reading this tale as I turn the pages once more . . .

The forest-girdled village upon the Jura slopes slept soundly, although it was not yet many minutes after ten o'clock. The clang of the *couvre-feu* had indeed just ceased, its notes swept far into the woods by a wind that shook the mountains. This wind now rushed down the deserted street. It howled about the old rambling building called La Citadelle, whose roof towered gaunt and humped above the smaller houses—the Château left unfinished long ago by Lord Wemyss, the exiled Jacobite. The families who occupied the various apartments listened to the storm and felt the building tremble. 'It's the mountain wind. It will bring the snow,' the mother said, without looking up from her knitting. 'And how sad it sounds.'

But it was not the wind that brought sadness as we sat round the open fire of peat. It was the wind of memories. The lamplight slanted along the narrow room towards the table where breakfast things lay ready for the morning. The double windows were fastened. At the far end stood a door ajar, and on the other side of it the two elder children lay asleep in the big bed. But beside the window was a smaller unused bed, that had been empty now a year. And tonight was the anniversary. . . .

And so the wind brought sadness and long thoughts. The little chap that used to lie there was already twelve months gone, far, far beyond the Hole where the Winds came from, as he called it; yet it seemed only yesterday that I went to tell him a tuck-up story, to stroke Riquette, the old motherly cat that cuddled against his back and laid a paw beside his pillow like a human being, and to hear his funny little earnest whisper say, 'Oncle, tu sais, j'ai prié pour Petavel.' For La Citadelle had its unhappy ghost—of Petavel, the usurer, who had hanged himself in the attic a century gone by, and was known to walk its dreary corridors in search of peace—and this wise Irish mother, calming the boy's fears with wisdom, had told him, 'If you pray for Petavel, you'll save his soul and make him happy, and he'll only love you.' And, thereafter, this little imaginative boy had done so every night. With a passionate seriousness he did it. He had wonderful, delicate ways like that. In all our hearts he made his fairy nests of wonder. In my own, I know, he lay closer than any joy imaginable, with his big blue eyes, his queer soft questionings, and his splendid child's unselfishness—a sun-kissed flower of innocence that, had he lived, might have sweetened half a world.

'Let's put more peat on,' the mother said, as a handful of rain—like stones—came flinging against the windows; 'that must be hail.' And she went on tiptoe to the inner room. 'They're sleeping like two puddings,' she whispered, coming presently back. But it struck me she had taken longer than to notice merely that; and her face wore an odd expression that made me uncomfortable. I thought she was somehow just about to laugh or cry. By the table a second she hesitated. I caught the flash of indecision as it passed. 'Pan,' she said suddenly—it was a nickname, stolen from my tuck-up stories, *he* had given me—'I wonder how Riquette got in.' She looked hard at me. 'It wasn't you, was it?' For we never let her come at night since he had gone. It was too poignant. The beastie always went cuddling and nestling into that empty bed. But this time it was not my doing, and I offered plausible explanations. 'But—she's on the bed. Pan, *would* you be so kind——' She left the sentence unfinished, but I easily understood, for a lump had somehow risen in my own throat too, and I remembered now that she had come out from the inner room so quickly—with a kind of hurried rush almost. I put 'mère Riquette' out into the corridor. A lamp stood on the chair outside the door of another occupant further down, and I urged her gently towards it. She turned and looked at me—straight up into my face; instead of going down as I suggested, she went slowly in the opposite direction. She stepped softly towards a door in the wall that led up broken stairs into the attics. There she sat down and waited. And so I left her, and came back hastily to the peat fire and companionship. The wind rushed in behind me and slammed the door.

And we talked then somewhat busily of cheerful things; of the children's future, the excellence of the cheap Swiss schools, of Christmas presents, ski-ing, snow, tobogganing. I led the talk away from mournfulness; and when these subjects were exhausted I told stories of my own adventures in distant parts of the world. But 'mother' listened the whole time—not to me. Her thoughts were all elsewhere. And her air of intently, secretly listening, bordered, I felt, upon the uncanny. For she often stopped her knitting and sat with her eyes fixed upon the air before her; she stared blankly at the wall, her head slightly on one side, her figure tense, attention strained—elsewhere. Or, when my talk positively demanded it, her nod was oddly mechanical and her eyes looked through and past me. The wind continued very loud and roaring; but the fire glowed, the room was warm and cosy. Yet she shivered, and when I drew attention to it, her reply, 'I do feel cold, but I didn't know I shivered,' was given as though she spoke across the air to someone else. But what impressed me even more uncomfortably were her repeated questions about Riquette. When a pause in my tales permitted, she would look up with 'I wonder where Riquette went?' or, thinking of the inclement night, 'I hope mère Riquette's not out of doors. Perhaps Madame Favre has taken her in?' I offered to go and see. Indeed I was already half-way across the room when there came the heavy bang at the door that rooted me to the ground where I stood. It was not wind. It was something alive that made it rattle. There was a second blow. A thud on the corridor boards followed, and then a high, odd voice that at first was as human as the cry of a child.

It is undeniable that we both started, and for myself I can answer truthfully that a chill ran down my spine; but what frightened me more than the sudden noise and the eerie cry was the way 'mother' supplied the immediate explanation. For behind the words 'It's only Riquette; she sometimes springs at the door like that; perhaps we'd better let her in,' was a certain touch of uncanny quiet that made me feel she had known the cat would come, and knew also *why* she came. One cannot explain such impressions further. They leave their vital touch, then go their way. Into the little room, however, in that moment there came between us this uncomfortable sense that the night held other purposes than our own—and that my companion was aware of them. There was something going on far, far removed from the routine of life as we were accustomed to it. Moreover, our usual routine was the eddy, while this was the main stream. It felt big, I mean.

And so it was that the entrance of the familiar, friendly creature brought this thing both itself and 'mother' *knew*, but whereof I as yet was ignorant. I held the door wide. The draught rushed through behind her, and sent a shower of sparks about the fireplace. The lamp flickered and gave a little gulp. And Riquette marched slowly past, with all the impressive dignity of her kind, towards the other door that stood ajar. Turning the corner like a shadow, she disappeared into the room where the two children slept. We heard the soft thud with which she leaped upon the bed. Then, in a lull of the wind, she came back again and sat on the oilcloth, staring into 'mother's' face. She mewed and put a paw out, drawing the black dress softly with half-opened claws. And it was all so horribly suggestive and pathetic, it revived such poignant memories, that I got up impulsively—I think I had actually said the words, 'We'd better put her out, mother, after all'—when my companion rose to her feet and forestalled me. She said another thing instead. It took my breath away to hear it. 'She wants us to go with her. Pan, will you come too?' The surprise on my face must have asked the question, for I do not remember saying anything. 'To the attic,' she said quietly.

She stood there by the table, a tall, grave figure dressed in black, and her face above the lamp-shade caught the full glare of light. Its expression positively stiffened me. She seemed so secure in her singular purpose. And her familiar appearance had so oddly given place to something wholly strange to me. She looked like another person—almost with the unwelcome transformation of the sleep-walker about her. Cold came over me as I watched her, for I remembered suddenly her Irish second-sight, her story years ago of meeting a figure on the attic stairs, the figure of Petavel. And the idea of this motherly, sedate, and wholesome woman, absorbed day and night in prosaic domestic duties, and yet 'seeing' things, touched the incongruous almost to the point of alarm. It was so distressingly convincing.

Yet she knew quite well that I would come. Indeed, following the excited animal, she was already by the door, and a moment later, still without answering or protesting, I was with them in the draughty corridor. There was something inevitable in her manner that made it impossible to refuse.

She took the lamp from its nail on the wall, and following our four-footed guide, who ran with obvious pleasure just in front, she opened the door into the courtyard. The wind nearly put the lamp out, but a minute later we were safe inside the passage that led up flights of creaky wooden stairs towards the world of tenantless attics overhead.

And I shall never forget the way the excited Riquette first stood up and put her paws upon the various doors, trotted ahead, turned back to watch us coming, and then finally sat down and waited on the threshold of the empty, raftered space that occupied the entire length of the building underneath the roof. For her manner was more that of an intelligent dog than of a cat, and sometimes more like that of a human mind than either.

We had come up without a single word. The howling of the wind as we rose higher was like the roar of artillery. There were many broken stairs, and the narrow way was full of twists and turnings. It was a dreadful journey. I felt eyes watching us from all the yawning spaces of the darkness, and the noise of the storm smothered footsteps everywhere. Troops of shadows kept us company. But it was on the threshold of this big, chief attic, when 'mother' stopped abruptly to put down the lamp, that real fear took hold of me. For Riquette marched steadily forward into the middle of the dusty flooring, picking her way among the fallen tiles and mortar, as though she went towards—someone. She purred loudly and uttered little cries of excited pleasure. Her tail went up into the air, and she lowered her head with the unmistakable intention of being stroked. Her lips opened and shut. Her green eyes smiled. She *was* being stroked.

It was an unforgettable performance. I would rather have witnessed an execution or a murder than watch that mysterious creature twist and turn about in the way she did. Her magnified shadow was as large as a pony on the floor and rafters. I wanted to hide the whole thing by extinguishing the lamp. For, even before the mysterious action began, I experienced the sudden rush of conviction that others besides ourselves were in this attic—and standing very close to us indeed. And, although there was ice in my blood, there was also a strange swelling of the heart that only love and tenderness could bring.

But, whatever it was, my human companion, still silent, knew and understood. She *saw*. And her soft whisper that ran with the wind among the rafters, 'Il a prié pour Petavel et le bon Dieu l'a entendu,' did not amaze me one quarter as much as the expression I then caught upon her radiant face. Tears ran down the cheeks, but they were tears of happiness. Her whole figure seemed lit up. She opened her arms—picture of great Motherhood, proud, blessed, and tender beyond words. I thought she was going to fall, for she took quick steps forward; but when I moved to catch her, she drew me aside instead with a sudden gesture that brought fear back in the place of wonder.

'Let them pass,' she whispered grandly. 'Pan, don't you see. . . . He's leading him into peace and safety . . . by the hand!' And her joy seemed to kill the shadows and fill the entire attic with white light. Then, almost simultaneously with her words, she swayed. I was in time to catch her, but as I did so, across the very spot where we had just been standing—two figures, I swear, went past us like a flood of light.

There was a moment next of such confusion that I did not see what happened to Riquette, for the sight of my companion kneeling on the dusty boards and praying with a curious sort of passionate happiness, while tears pressed between her covering fingers—the strange wonder of this made me utterly oblivious to minor details. . . .

We were sitting round the peat fire again, and 'mother' was saying to me in the gentlest, tenderest whisper I ever heard from human lips—'Pan, I think perhaps that's why God took him. . . .'

And when a little later we went in to make Riquette cosy in the empty bed, ever since kept sacred to her use, the mournfulness had lifted; and in the place of resignation was proud peace and joy that knew no longer sad or selfish questionings.

The Thing in the Cellar

DAVID H. KELLER

From the attic it is not too far a journey to step down into the cellar—and again I expect most readers have some experience of their dark depths and the strange noises that are suddenly heard there and are never very easy to explain. Of course with the lights on, cellars can seem like an Aladdin's cave full of treasures and mementoes from the past, but shrouded in darkness they seem the very haunt of mystery. This is the theme which David H. Keller, the American fantasy and science fiction writer, explores in "The Thing in the Cellar" and it is a doubly interesting tale in that the author was himself a doctor and made a particular study of subconscious fears. The cellar which so frightens Tommy Tucker is not one that I should care to get too near myself.

It was a large cellar, entirely out of proportion to the house above it. The owner admitted that it was probably built for a distinctly different kind of structure from the one which rose above it. Probably the first house had been burned, and poverty had caused a diminution of the dwelling erected to take its place.

A winding stone stairway connected the cellar with the kitchen. Around the base of this series of steps successive owners of the house had placed their firewood, winter vegetables and junk. The junk had gradually been pushed back till it rose, head high, in a barricade of uselessness. What was at the back of that barricade no one knew and no one cared. For some hundreds of years no one had crossed it to penetrate to the black reaches of the cellar behind it.

At the top of the steps, separating the kitchen from the cellar, was a stout oaken door. This door was, in a way, as peculiar and out of relation to the rest of the house as the cellar itself. It was a strange kind of door to find in a modern house, and certainly a most unusual door to find in the inside of the house—thick, stoutly built, dextrously rabbeted together, with huge wrought-iron hinges, and a lock that looked as though it came from Castle Despair. Separating a house from the outside world, such a door would be excusable; swinging between kitchen and cellar it seemed particularly inappropriate.

From the earliest months of his life Tommy Tucker seemed unhappy in the kitchen. In the front parlour, in the formal dining-room, and especially on the second floor of the house he acted like a normal, healthy child; but carry him to the kitchen, and he at once began to cry. His parents, being plain people, ate in the kitchen save when they had company. Being poor, Mrs Tucker did most of her work, though she occasionally had a charwoman in to do the extra Saturday cleaning, and thus much of her time was spent in the kitchen. And Tommy stayed with her, at least as long as he was unable to walk. Much of the time he was decidedly unhappy.

When Tommy learned to creep, he lost no time in leaving the kitchen. No sooner was his mother's back turned than the little fellow crawled as fast as he could for the doorway opening into the front of the house, the dining-room and the front parlour. Once away from the kitchen, he seemed happy; at least he ceased to cry. On being returned to the kitchen his howls so thoroughly convinced the neighbours that he had colic that more than one bowl of catnip and sage tea was brought to his assistance.

It was not until the boy learned to talk that the Tuckers had any idea as to what made the boy cry so hard when he was in the kitchen. In other words, the baby had to suffer for many months till he obtained at least a little relief, and even when he told his parents what was the matter, they were absolutely unable to comprehend. This is not to be wondered at, because they were both hard-working, rather simple-minded persons.

What they finally learned from their little son was this: that if the cellar door was shut and securely fastened with the heavy iron lock, Tommy could at least eat a meal in peace. If the door was simply closed and not locked, he shivered with fear, but kept quiet. But if the door was open, if even the slightest streak of black showed that it was not tightly shut, then the little three-year-old would scream himself to the point of exhaustion, especially if his tired father would refuse him permission to leave the kitchen.

Playing in the kitchen, the child developed two interesting habits. Rags, scraps of paper and splinters of wood were continually being shoved under the thick oak door to fill the space between the door and the sill. Whenever Mrs Tucker opened the door there was always some trash there, placed by her son. It annoyed her, and more than once the little fellow was thrashed for this conduct, but punishment acted in no way as a deterrent.

The other habit was as singular. Once the door was closed and locked, he would rather boldly walk over to it and caress the old lock. Even when he was so small that he had to stand on tiptoe to touch it with the tips of his fingers he would touch it with slow caressing strokes; later on, as he grew, he used to kiss it.

His father, who only saw the boy at the end of the day, decided that there was no sense in such conduct, and in his masculine way tried to break the lad of his foolishness. There was, of necessity, no effort on the part of the hard-working man to understand the psychology behind his son's conduct. All that the man knew was that his little son was acting in a way that was decidedly queer.

Tommy loved his mother and was willing to do anything he could to help her in the household chores, but one thing he would not do, and never do, and that was to fetch and carry between the house and the cellar. If his mother opened the door, he would run screaming from the room, and he never returned voluntarily until he was assured that the door was closed.

He never explained just why he acted as he did. In fact, he refused to talk about it, at least to his parents, and that was just as well, because had he done so, they would simply have been more positive than ever that there was something radically wrong with their only child. They tried, in their own ways, to break the child of his unusual habits; failing to change him at all, they decided to ignore his peculiarities. That is, they ignored them until he became six years old and the time came for him to go to school. He was a sturdy little chap by that time, and more intelligent than the usual boys beginning in the primer class. Mr Tucker was, at times, proud of him; the child's attitude towards the cellar door was the one thing most disturbing to the father's pride. Finally nothing would do but that the Tucker family call on the neighbourhood physician. It was an important event in the life of the Tuckers, so important that it demanded the wearing of Sunday clothes.

'The matter is just this, Doctor Hawthorne,' said Mr Tucker, in a somewhat embarrassed manner. 'Our little Tommy is old enough to start school, but he behaves childish in regard to our cellar, and the missus and I thought you could tell us how to do about it. It must be his nerves.'

'Ever since he was a baby,' continued Mrs Tucker, taking up the thread of conversation where her husband had paused, 'Tommy has had a great fear of the cellar. Even now, big boy that he is, he does not love me enough to fetch and carry for me through that door and down those steps. It is not natural for a child to act like he does, and what with chinking the cracks with rags and kissing the lock, he drives me to the point where I fear he may become daft-like as he grows older.'

The doctor, eager to satisfy new customers, and dimly remembering some lecture on the nervous system which he'd attended when he was a medical student, asked some general questions, listened to the boy's heart, examined his lungs and looked at his eyes and fingernails. At last he commented: 'Looks like a fine, healthy boy to me.'

'Yes, all except the cellar door,' replied the father.

'Has he ever been sick?'

'Naught but fits once or twice when he cried himself blue in the face,' answered the mother.

'Frightened?'

'Perhaps. It was always in the kitchen.'

'Suppose you go out and let me talk to Tommy by myself?'

And there sat the doctor very much at his ease and the little six-year-old boy very uneasy.

'Tommy, what is there in the cellar you are afraid of?' the doctor asked.

'I don't know.'

'Have you seen it?'

'No, sir.'

'Ever heard it? smelt it?'

'No, sir.'

'Then how do you know there is something there?'

'Because.'

'Because what?'

'Because there is.'

That was as far as Tommy would go, and at last his seeming obstinacy annoyed the physician even as it had for several years annoyed Mr Tucker. He went to the door and called the parents into the office.

'He thinks there is something down in the cellar,' he stated.

The Tuckers simply looked at each other.

'That's foolish,' commented Mr Tucker.

' 'Tis just a plain cellar with junk and firewood and cider barrels in it,' added Mrs Tucker. 'Since we moved into that house, I have not missed a day without going down those stone steps and I know there is nothing there. But the lad has always screamed when the door was open. I recall now that since he was a child in arms he has always screamed when the door was open.'

'He thinks there is something there,' said the doctor.

'That is why we brought him to you,' replied the father. 'It's the child's nerves. Perhaps soothing syrup, or something, will calm him.'

'I tell you what to do,' advised the doctor. 'He thinks there is something there. Just as soon as he finds that he is wrong and that there is nothing there, he will forget about it. He has been humoured too much. What you want to do is to open that cellar door and make him stay by himself in the kitchen. Nail the door open so he can not close it. Leave him alone there for an hour and then go and laugh at him and show him how silly it was for him to be afraid of an empty cellar. I will give you some nerve and blood tonic and that will help, but the big thing is to show him that there is nothing to be afraid of.'

On the way back to the Tucker home Tommy broke away from his parents. They caught him after an exciting chase and kept him between them the rest of the way home. Once in the house he disappeared and was found in the guest room under the bed. The afternoon being already spoiled for Mr Tucker, he determined to keep the child under observation for the rest of the day. Tommy ate no supper, in spite of the urgings of the unhappy mother. The dishes were washed, the evening paper read, the evening pipe smoked; and then, and only then, did Mr Tucker take down his tool box and get out a hammer and some long nails.

'And I am going to nail the door open, Tommy, so you cannot close it, as that was what the doctor said, Tommy, and you are to be a man and stay here in the kitchen for an hour, and we will leave the lamp a-burning, and then when you find there is naught to be afraid of, you will be well and a real man and not something for a man to be ashamed of being the father of.'

But at the last Mrs Tucker kissed Tommy and cried and whispered to her husband not to do it, and to wait till the boy was larger. But nothing was to do but to nail the thick door open so it could not be shut and leave the boy there with the lamp burning and the dark open space of the doorway to look at with eyes that grew as hot and burning as the flame of the lamp.

That same day Doctor Hawthorne took supper with a

classmate of his, a man who specialised in psychiatry and who was particularly interested in children. Hawthorne told Johnson about his newest case, the little Tucker boy, and asked him for his opinion.

Johnson frowned. 'Children are odd, Hawthorne. Perhaps they are like dogs. It may be their nervous system is more acute than it is in the adult. We know that our eyesight is limited, also our hearing and sense of smell. I firmly believe that there are forms of life which exist in such a form that we can neither see, hear nor smell them. Fondly we delude ourselves into the fallacy of believing that they do not exist because we cannot prove their existence.

'This Tucker lad may have a nervous system that is peculiarly acute. He may dimly appreciate the existence of something in the cellar which is unappreciable to his parents. Evidently there is some basis to this fear of his. Now, I am not saying that there is anything in the cellar. In fact, I suppose that it is just an ordinary cellar, but this boy, since he was a baby, has thought there was something there, and that is just as bad as though there actually were. What I would like to know is what makes him think so. Give me the address, and I will call tomorrow and have a talk with the little fellow.'

'What do you think of my advice?'

'Sorry, old man, but I think it was perfectly rotten. If I were you I would stop around there on my way home and prevent them from following it. The little fellow may be badly frightened. You see, he evidently thinks there is something there.'

'But there isn't.'

'Perhaps not. No doubt he is wrong, but he thinks so.'

It all worried Doctor Hawthorne so much that he decided to take his friend's advice. It was a damp night, a foggy night, and the physician felt cold as he tramped along the city streets. At last he came to the Tucker house. There was a light in the front window, and in no time at all Mr Tucker came to the door.

'I have come to see Tommy,' said the doctor.

'He is back in the kitchen,' replied the father.

'He gave one cry, but since then he has been quiet,' sobbed the wife.

'If I had let her have her way, she would have opened the door, but I said to her, "Mother, now is the time to make a man out of our Tommy." And I guess he knows by now that there was naught to be afraid of. Well, the hour is up. Suppose we go and get him and put him to bed?'

'It has been a hard time for the little child,' whispered the wife.

Carrying the candle, the man walked ahead of the woman and the doctor, and at last opened the kitchen door. The room was dark.

'Lamp has gone out,' said the man. 'Wait till I light it.'

'Tommy! Tommy!' called Mrs Tucker.

But the doctor ran to where a white form was stretched on the floor. Sharply he called for more light. Trembling, he examined all that was left of little Tommy. Twitching, he looked into the open space down into the cellar. At last he looked at Tucker and Tucker's wife.

'Tommy—Tommy has been hurt. I guess he is dead!' he stammered.

The mother threw herself on the floor and picked up the torn, mutilated thing that had been, only a short while ago, her little Tommy.

The man took his hammer and drew out the nails and closed the door and locked it and then drove in a long spike to reinforce the lock. Then he took hold of the doctor's shoulders and shook him.

'What killed him, Doctor? What killed him?' he shouted into Hawthorne's ear.

The doctor looked at him bravely in spite of the fear in his throat.

'How do I know, Tucker?' he replied. 'How do I know? Didn't you tell me that there was nothing there? Nothing down there? In the cellar?'

The Dabblers

W. F. HARVEY

Many teachers have been interested in the "secret world" of schoolchildren. Professor M. R. James, the author of the first story, for instance, was particularly fascinated by the strange little rituals that children had devised for their own purposes and saw how they were passed down by word of mouth from generation to generation. Many of these rites were harmless enough games testing strength or courage, but there were others of a rather sinister nature. W. F. Harvey, the author of "The Dabblers", spent a number of years in education, and was similarly attracted to the gossip and rumours he heard of secret societies run by the young. In fact in the introduction to one of his collections of stories there is mention of a group of sixth formers at a preparatory school who worshipped a god called Lar—the God of the Hearth—by sacrificing beetles to him at midnight ceremonies. It was this kind of report which inspired him to write "The Dabblers"— which not only sounds authentic but is tinged with just the right amount of the bizarre to send a shudder up the spine . . .

It was a wet July evening. The three friends sat around the peat fire in Harborough's den, pleasantly weary after their long tramp across the moors. Scott, the ironmaster, had been declaiming against modern education. His partner's son had recently entered the business with everything to learn, and the business couldn't afford to teach him. 'I suppose,' he said, 'that from preparatory school to university, Wilkins must have spent the best of three thousand pounds on filling a suit of plus-fours with brawn. It's too much. My boy is going to Steelborough grammar school. Then when he's sixteen I shall send him to Germany so that he can learn from our competitors. Then he'll put in a year in the office; afterwards, if he shows any ability, he can go up to Oxford. Of course he'll be rusty and out of his stride, but he can mug up his Latin in the evenings as my shop stewards do with their industrial history and economics.'

'Things aren't as bad as you make out,' said Freeman, the architect. 'The trouble I find with schools is in choosing the right one where so many are excellent. I've entered my boy for one of those old country grammar schools that have been completely remodelled. Wells showed in *The Undying Fire* what an enlightened headmaster can do when he is given a free hand and isn't buried alive in mortar and tradition.'

'You'll probably find,' said Scott, 'that it's mostly eyewash; no discipline, and a lot of talk about self-expression and education for service.'

'There you're wrong. I should say the discipline is too severe if anything. I heard only the other day from my young nephew that two boys had been expelled for a raid on a hen-roost or some such escapade; but I suppose there was more to it than met the eye. What are you smiling about, Harborough?'

'It was something you said about headmasters and tradition. I was thinking about tradition and boys. Rum, secretive little beggars. It seems to me quite possible that there is a wealth of hidden lore passed on from one generation of schoolboys to another that it might be well worth while for a psychologist or an anthropologist to investigate. I remember at my first school writing some lines of doggerel in my books. They were really an imprecation against anyone who should steal them. I've seen practically the same words in old monkish manuscripts; they go back to the time when books were of value. But it was on the fly-leaves of Abbott's *Via Latina* and Lock's *Arithmetic* that I wrote them. Nobody would want to steal those books. Why should boys start to spin tops at a certain season of the year? The date is not fixed by shopkeepers, parents are not consulted, and though saints have been flogged to death I have found no connection between top whipping and the church calendar. The matter is decided for them by an unbroken tradition, handed down, not from father to son, but from boy to boy. Nursery rhymes are not perhaps a case in point, though they are stuffed with odd bits of folklore. I remember being taught a game that was played with knotted handkerchiefs manipulated by the fingers to the accompaniment of a rhyme which began: "Father Confessor, I've come to confess." My instructor, aged eight, was the son of a High Church vicar. I don't know what would have happened if old Tomlinson had heard the last verse:

> "Father Confessor, what shall I do?"
> "Go to Rome and kiss the Pope's toe."
> "Father Confessor, I'd rather kiss you."
> "Well, child, do." '

'What was the origin of that little piece of doggerel?' asked Freeman. 'It's new to me.'

'I don't know,' Harborough replied. 'I've never seen it in print. But behind the noddings of the knotted handkerchiefs and our childish giggles lurked something sinister. I seem to see the cloaked figure, cat-like and gliding, of one of those emissaries of the Church of Rome that creep into the pages of George Borrow—hatred and fear masked in ribaldry. I could give you other examples, the holly and ivy carols, for instance, which used to be sung by boys and girls to the accompaniment of a dance, and which, according to some people, embody a crude form of nature worship.'

'And the point of all this is what?' asked Freeman.

'That there is a body of tradition, ignored by the ordinary adult, handed down by one generation of children to another. If you want a really good example—a really bad example I should say, I'll tell you the story of the Dabblers.' He waited until Freeman and Scott had filled their pipes and then began.

'When I came down from Oxford and before I was called to the Bar, I put in three miserable years at school teaching.'

Scott laughed.

'I don't envy the poor kids you cross-examined,' he said. 'As a matter of fact, I was more afraid of them than they of me. I got a job as usher at one of Freeman's old grammar schools, only it had not been remodelled and the headmaster was a completely incompetent cleric. It was in the eastern counties. The town was dead-alive. The only thing that seemed to warm the hearts of the people there was a dull smouldering fire of gossip, and they all took turns in fanning the flame. But I mustn't get away from the school. The buildings were old; the chapel had once been the choir of a monastic church. There was a fine tithe barn, and a few old stones and bases of pillars in the headmaster's garden, but nothing more to show where monks had lived for centuries except a dried-up fish pond.

'Late in June at the end of my first year, I was crossing the playground at night on my way to my lodgings in the High Street. It was after twelve. There wasn't a breath of air, and the playing fields were covered with a thick mist from the river. There was something rather weird about the whole scene; it was all so still and silent. The night smelt stuffy; and then suddenly I heard the sound of singing. I don't know where the voices came from nor how many voices there were, and not being musical I can't give you any idea of the tune. It was very ragged with gaps in it, and there was something about it which I can only describe as disturbing. Anyhow I had no desire to investigate. I stood still for two or three minutes listening and then let myself out by the lodge gate into the deserted High Street. My bedroom above the tobacconist's looked out on to a lane that led down to the river. Through the open window I could still hear, very faintly, the singing. Then a dog began to howl, and when after a quarter of an hour it stopped, the June night was again still. Next morning in the masters' common room I asked if anyone could account for the singing.

' "It's the Dabblers," said old Moneypenny, the science master, "they usually appear about now."

'Of course I asked who the Dabblers were.

' "The Dabblers," said Moneypenny, "are carol singers born out of their due time. They are certain lads of the village who, for reasons of their own, desire to remain anonymous; probably choir-boys with a grievance, who wish to pose as ghosts. And for goodness' sake let sleeping dogs lie. We've thrashed out the Dabbler controversy so often that I'm heartily sick of it."

'He was a cross-grained customer and I took him at his word. But later on in the week I got hold of one of the junior masters and asked him what it all meant. It seemed an established fact that the singing did occur at this particular time of the year. It was a sore point with Moneypenny, because on one occasion when somebody had suggested that it might be boys from the schoolhouse skylarking he had completely lost his temper.

' "All the same," said Atkinson, "it might just as well be our boys as any others. If you are game next year we'll try to get to the bottom of it."

'I agreed and there the matter stood. As a matter of fact when the anniversary came round I had forgotten all about the thing. I had been taking the lower school in prep. The boys had been unusually restless—we were less than a month from the end of term—and it was with a sigh of relief that I turned into Atkinson's study soon after eight to borrow an umbrella, for it was raining hard.

' "By the by," he said, "tonight's the night the Dabblers are due to appear. What about it?"

'I told him that if he imagined that I was going to spend the hours between then and midnight in patrolling the school precincts in the rain, he was greatly mistaken.

' "That's not my idea at all," he said. "We won't set foot out of doors. I'll light the fire; I can manage a mixed grill of sorts on the gas ring and there are a couple of bottles of beer in the cupboard. If we hear the Dabblers we'll quietly go the round of the dormitories and see if anyone is missing. If they are, we can await their return."

'The long and short of it was that I fell in with his proposal.

I had a lot of essays to correct on the Peasants' Revolt—fancy kids of thirteen and fourteen being expected to write essays on anything—and I could go through them just as well by Atkinson's fire as in my own cheerless little sitting-room.

'It's wonderful how welcome a fire can be in a sodden June. We forgot our lost summer as we sat beside it smoking, warming our memories in the glow from the embers.

' "Well," said Atkinson at last, "it's close on twelve. If the Dabblers are going to start, they are due about now." He got up from his chair and drew aside the curtains.

' "Listen!" he said. Across the playground, from the direction of the playing-fields, came the sound of singing. The music—if it could be called such—lacked melody and rhythm and was broken by pauses; it was veiled, too, by the drip, drip of the rain and the splashing of water from the gutter spouts. For one moment I thought I saw lights moving, but my eyes must have been deceived by reflections on the window pane.

' "We'll see if any of our birds have flown," said Atkinson. He picked up an electric torch and we went the rounds of the dormitories. Everything was as it should be. The beds were all occupied, the boys all seemed to be asleep. It was a quarter-past twelve by the time we got back to Atkinson's room. The music had ceased; I borrowed a mackintosh and ran home through the rain.

'That was the last time I heard the Dabblers, but I was to hear of them again. Act II was staged up at Scapa. I'd been transferred to a hospital ship, with a dislocated shoulder for X-ray, and as luck would have it the right-hand cot to mine was occupied by a lieutenant, R.N.V.R., a fellow called Holster, who had been at old Edmed's school a year or two before my time. From him I learned a little more about the Dabblers. It seemed that they were boys who for some reason or other kept up a school tradition. Holster thought that they got out of the house by means of the big wisteria outside B dormitory, after leaving carefully constructed dummies in their beds. On the night in June when the Dabblers were due to appear it was considered bad form to stay awake too long and very unhealthy to ask too many questions, so that the identity of the Dabblers remained a mystery. To the big and burly Holster there was nothing really mysterious about the thing; it was a schoolboys' lark and nothing more. An unsatisfactory act, you will agree, and one which fails to carry the story forward. But with the third act the drama begins to move. You see I had the good luck to meet one of the Dabblers in the flesh.

'Burlingham was badly shell-shocked in the war; a psychoanalyst took him in hand and he made a seemingly miraculous recovery. Then two years ago he had a partial relapse, and when I met him at Lady Byfleet's he was going up to town three times a week for special treatment from some unqualified West End practitioner, who seemed to be getting at the root of the trouble. There was something extraordinarily likeable about the man. He had a whimsical sense of humour that must have been his salvation, and with it was combined a capacity for intense indignation that one doesn't often meet with these days. We had a number of interesting talks together (part of his regime consisted of long cross-country walks, and he was glad enough of a companion) but the one I naturally remember was when in a tirade against English educational methods he mentioned Dr Edmed's name—"the head of a beastly little grammar school where I spent five of the most miserable years of my life."

' "Three more than I did," I replied.

' "Good God!" he said, "fancy you being a product of that place!"

' "I was one of the producers," I answered. "I'm not proud of the fact; I usually keep it dark."

' "There was a lot too much kept dark about that place," said Burlingham. It was the second time he had used the words. As he uttered them, "that place" sounded almost the equivalent of an unnameable hell. We talked for a time about the school, of Edmed's pomposity, of old Jacobson the porter —a man whose patient good humour shone alike on the just and on the unjust—of the rat hunts in the tithe barn on the last afternoons of term.

' "And now," I said at last, "tell me about the Dabblers."

'He turned round on me like a flash and burst out laughing, a high-pitched, nervous laugh that, remembering his condition, made me sorry I had introduced the subject.

' "How damnably funny!" he said. "The man I go to in town asked me the same question only a fortnight ago. I broke an oath in telling him, but I don't see why you shouldn't know as well. Not that there is anything to know; it's all a queer boyish nightmare without rhyme or reason. You see I was one of the Dabblers myself."

'It was a curious disjointed story that I got out of Burlingham. The Dabblers were a little society of five, sworn on solemn oath to secrecy. On a certain night in June, after warning had been given by their leader, they climbed out of the dormitories and met by the elm-tree in old Edmed's garden. A raid was made on the doctor's poultry run, and, having secured a fowl, they retired to the tithe barn, cut its throat, plucked and cleaned it, and then roasted it over a fire in a brazier while the rats looked on. The leader of the Dabblers produced sticks of incense; he lit his own from the fire, the others kindling theirs from his. Then all moved in slow procession to the summer-house in the corner of the doctor's garden, singing as they went. There was no sense in the words they sang They weren't English and they weren't Latin. Burlingham described them as reminding him of the refrain in the old nursery rhyme:

> There were three brothers over the sea,
> *Peri meri dixi domine.*
> They sent three presents unto me,
> *Petrum partrum paradisi tempore*
> *Peri meri dixi domine.*

' "And that was all?" I said to him.

' "Yes," he replied, "that was all there was to it; but——"

'I expected the but.

' "We were all of us frightened, horribly frightened. It was quite different from the ordinary schoolboy escapade. And yet there was fascination, too, in the fear. It was rather like," and here he laughed, "dragging a deep pool for the body of someone who had been drowned. You didn't know who it was, and you wondered what would turn up."

'I asked him a lot of questions but he hadn't anything very definite to tell me. The Dabblers were boys in the lower and middle forms and with the exception of the leader their membership of the fraternity was limited to two years. Quite a number of the boys, according to Burlingham, must have been Dabblers, but they never talked about it and no one, as far as he knew, had broken his oath. The leader in his time was called Tancred, the most unpopular boy in the school, despite the fact that he was their best athlete. He was expelled following an incident that took place in chapel. Burlingham didn't know what it was; he was away in the sick-room at the time, and the accounts, I gather, varied considerably.'

Harborough broke off to fill his pipe.

'Act IV will follow immediately,' he said.

'All this is very interesting,' observed Scott, 'but I'm afraid that if it's your object to curdle our blood you haven't quite succeeded. And if you hope to spring a surprise on us in Act IV we must disillusion you.' Freeman nodded assent.

' "Scott who Edgar Wallace read," ' he began. 'We're familiar nowadays with the whole bag of tricks. Black Mass is a certain winner; I put my money on him. Go on, Harborough.'

'You don't give a fellow half a chance, but I suppose you're right. Act IV takes place in the study of the Rev. Montague Cuttler, vicar of St Mary Parbeloe, a former senior mathematics master, but before Edmed's time—a dear old boy, blind as a bat, and a Fellow of the Society of Antiquaries. He knew nothing about the Dabblers. He wouldn't. But he knew a very great deal about the past history of the school, when it wasn't a school but a monastery. He used to do a little quiet excavating in the vacations and had discovered what he believed to be the stone that marked the tomb of Abbot Polegate. The man, it appeared, had a bad reputation for dabbling in forbidden mysteries.'

'Hence the name Dabblers, I suppose,' said Scott.

'I'm not so sure,' Harborough answered. 'I think that more probably it's derived from *diabolos*. But, anyhow, from old Cuttler I gathered that the abbot's stone was where Edmed had placed his summer-house. Now doesn't it all illustrate my theory beautifully? I admit that there are no thrills in the story. There's nothing really supernatural about it. Only it does show the power of oral tradition when you think of a bastard form of the black mass surviving like this for hundreds of years under the very noses of the pedagogues.'

'It shows too,' said Freeman, 'what we have to suffer from incompetent headmasters. Now at the place I was telling you about where I've entered my boy—and I wish I could show you their workshops and art rooms—they've got a fellow who is——'

'What was the name of the school?' interrupted Harborough.

'Whitechurch Abbey.'

'And a fortnight ago, you say, two boys were expelled for a raid on a hen roost?'

'Yes.'

'Well, it's the same place that I've been talking about. The Dabblers were out.'

'Act V,' said Scott, 'and curtain. Harborough, you've got your thrill after all.'

The Tortoise-Shell Cat

GREYE LA SPINA

It is not just boys who have a monopoly on strange and secret rites, schoolgirls similarly have their own world of mystery which they keep closely guarded from the eyes of teachers and parents. In "The Tortoise-Shell Cat", however, the popular American fantasy writer Greye La Spina is not so much interested in the rites of a group of children, but rather the peculiar powers of one small girl who has just recently arrived at an American boarding school. The girl, Vida di Monserreau, obviously possesses occult powers of some kind, and as the occult is not something to be taken lightly, those who cross her path find themselves in considerable peril. Miss La Spina retells her story in a series of letters which dramatically introduce us to a most sinister night creature indeed.

Extract from a letter from Althea Benedict, Pine Valley Academy for Young Ladies, to Mrs Wordsworth Benedict, New York City:

In spite of your care to reserve a room for me, Miss Annette Lee called me into her office yesterday and begged me to share it with a new girl.

It seems that Vida is the only child of a very old friend of hers, Felix di Monserreau, a rich Louisiana planter. Miss Lee says she thinks I may have a good influence over my new room-mate, but she managed to evade my tactful inquiry as to what Vida's vices might be. She did seem awfully disturbed. She said that she appreciated my nice attitude; and if I found the companionship disturbed me, would I report it to her immediately? She was so agitated she just couldn't look me in the face. I can't imagine what can be the matter with Vida.

So far, my new room-mate appears to be rather nice. Her father has been most generous and our room is the envy of all the other girls. I would have written you earlier, mother, but we've been getting our new things settled.

Vida wants everything to go with her particular style of beauty! She confessed that she was perfectly miserable if she didn't have a background that suited her, and that she knew I wouldn't mind—particularly as she was willing to pay for the decorations. So she has the room decorated in the most stunning fashion, in shades of orange and dull green, with heaps and heaps of down-cushions. She says she loves to lie around on a pile of cushions, like a cat.

I wish you could see her. She's really a type of girl to attract attention anywhere with her deadwhite skin, her dark red lips, her black hair and her eyes——. Her eyes are quite the queerest I've ever seen. They are narrow, long, slumbrous, with drooping lids through which she looks at one in her peculiar way. The iris is a kind of pale golden-brown that gives the impression of warm yellow. When dusk comes, I've seen the pupil glowing with some strange iridescence, the iris a narrow yellow rim about it; for all the world, it makes me think of a cat's eye.

Don't forget to tell Cousin Edgar to send me the necklace he promised to bring me from Egypt. I've told the girls about it, and they're dying to see it.

YOUR ALTHEA.

The same to the same:

... Studies are going forward nicely. Nothing new, except a couple of rather queer things about my room-mate. I thought I'd better write to you first, before saying anything to Miss Lee about it. Perhaps I'm only imagining things, anyway.

Vida is certainly a very odd girl, mother. I am beginning to believe that she can see in the dark, with those strange eyes of hers. What makes me think so—you know how I love to change furniture around every little while? The other day I altered the position of everything in the room. Vida wasn't there, and before she came back the 'lights-out' bell rang. I meant to stay awake and tell her not to fall over the table that was in front of her bed, but when she did come I was so drowsy that I didn't get a chance to speak to her before she had reached her bed.

And, mother, she threaded her way among those things just as if she could see them perfectly; not a single moment of hesitation. It gave me the most eerie feeling. I hid my head under the quilt, for I felt as if she were watching me in the dark. I know you'll laugh when you read this, but I didn't feel like laughing. And I still have an unpleasant feeling about it, for how could Vida walk so rapidly among those things, not one of which was in the same position she had seen them in last, unless she could actually see in the dark?

Last night another odd thing happened. There must have been crumbs in our waste-basket, for we heard a mouse rattling around in it. Just before I could switch on the light, I heard Vida bound across the room from her bed. When the light was on, she stood by the waste-basket with that mouse in her hands, and, I can tell you, it was a dead mouse! She looked so strange that I squeaked at her 'Vida!' She jumped, dropped the dead thing and scuttled back to bed. She seemed quite cross because I had put on the light, and I think she cried afterwards in the dark, although I can't be sure of it.

Mother, does it seem uncanny to you? I wonder if this night-sight is what Miss Annette referred to? I hate to say anything, for after all, what's the harm in it?

. . . When is Cousin Edgar going to send that necklace?

The same to the same:

. . . Something happened that I cannot help connecting with Vida. Yet I don't like to go to Miss Annette with it. I'm sure she will smile and tell me that I have an exceptionally lively imagination.

Vida and Natalie Cunningham had a dispute the other day about something or other, and Natalie looked it up and when she found Vida was right, she was sarcastic about it—

Natalie, I mean. Vida just looked at her with those strange golden eyes glowing, bit her lip, and remained silent.

When we were alone afterward, Vida said to me, 'Do you know, Althea, I'm afraid something unpleasant is going to happen to Natalie?'

I must have looked surprised, for she went on hastily:

'There's some kind of invisible guardian watching over me, Althea, that seems to know whenever anyone is unkind to me. For years I've observed that punishment is visited on everyone who crosses me or troubles me in any way. It has made me almost afraid of having a dispute with anyone, for if I permit myself—my real, inner-self—to grow disturbed, something always happens to the person at the root of the trouble.'

Of course, I hooted at her forebodings. I told her she was superstitious and silly. But, mother, that night Natalie Cunningham lost her favourite ring, a stunning emerald. It was stolen right off her dressing-table five minutes after Natalie turned off her light. She got up again to unlock the door for her room-mate, put on the light, and—the ring wasn't where she'd left it.

The door was still locked; the window was open but it was a third-storey window, as most of the dormitory windows in our buildings are, and there is no balcony under it.

Mysterious, wasn't it? Our floor monitor, Miss Poore, declared that Natalie must have dropped her ring on the floor, but Natalie has hunted and hunted. The ring certainly isn't in her room. Who took it? How? It frightened Natalie so that she is afraid to be alone in her room without a light.

The odd thing about it is the way that Vida looked at me when the girls told us about it. She actually wants me to believe that her 'invisible guardian' stole the ring to punish Natalie for having been sarcastic to her. Did you ever?

I wonder if poor Vida is—well, just a bit flighty, mother? How about that necklace?

The same to the same:

. . . I'm so excited that I can't write coherently. All the

school is in an uproar over what took place last night. I am more disturbed than the rest, for I am beginning to have a suspicion that Vida is right when she says that unpleasant things happen to people who cross her. It makes me nervous, for fear she may get provoked at me for something. I don't know whether or not I ought to report the whole thing to Miss Annette; I'm afraid she'll think I'm romancing. Won't you please write me and tell me what to do?

Yesterday morning Vida's old coloured mammy, Jinny, who is in Pine Valley in order to be near her charge, came up for Vida's laundry. Miss Poore came in while Vida was putting her soiled things together, and offered to help sort them over.

Mammy Jinny gave a kind of convulsive shiver. She looked up at Vida, staring hard at her for a moment. Vida stared back in a queer, fixed way. Then my room-mate's eyes flashed yellow fire. She told Miss Poore in a kind of fury that she'd better mind her own business and not stick her old-maid nose into other people's private concerns.

Miss Poore was wild. (You can't blame her. It was really nasty of Vida.) She took Vida by the shoulders and shook her hard. Vida didn't resist, but she looked at the floor monitor with such an expression of malice that Miss Poore actually stepped back in dismay.

'I'm sorry for you, Miss Poore,' said Vida to her. 'I'm afraid you are going to suffer severely for laying your hands on me. I'd save you if I could—but I can't.'

Miss Poore went out of the room without answering. Vida gave the laundry to Mammy Jinny, who insisted upon taking laundry-bag and all. After the old coloured woman had gone, Vida flung herself on her bed and cried for an hour. She said she was crying because she was sorry for Miss Poore. I failed at the time to see any significance in her remark, until after last night—.

About two o'clock this morning, the whole floor was wakened by the most terrible screams coming from Miss Poore's room. I sprang out of bed and rushed into the hall where I met the other girls, all pouring out of their rooms. We rushed to Miss Poore's room and she finally got her door open to let us in.

Mother, she was a sight! Face, hands, arms, were all covered with blood from bites and scratches. She was hysterical, and no wonder. She declared that some kind of wild animal had jumped in at her window and attacked her in the dark. The queer thing is, how did that creature—if there was one—get into her room and then out again before we opened the hall door? Her window was open, but it is a third-storey one and there is no tree near by from which an animal could have sprung into her room.

She is in such a condition this morning that Miss Annette told us in chapel she would have to leave the school to recover from the nervous shock incident to the attack. The mystery of it is the only topic of conversation today, as you can imagine. And now for the odd part of it.

When I got back to my room, there lay Vida, apparently sound asleep. She hadn't been disturbed by all that racket. Some sleeper! I woke her and told her.

Mother, she lay awake the rest of the night, crying and carrying on terribly, declaring it all her fault, although she couldn't help it. Her statement was rather confusing. She insisted it was her 'invisible guardian' who had attacked Miss Poore, but she begged me not to tell anyone. Her advice was superfluous; if I went to Miss Annette with such a statement, she'd think either Vida was crazy or I was simple.

I tried to sleep, but I can tell you I left the light on. And I wasn't the only one; all the girls had lights in their rooms the rest of the night.

The coincidences are strange, aren't they, mother? Natalie displeases Vida and has her emerald ring mysteriously stolen. Miss Poore displeases Vida and gets scratched and bitten. But even a coincidence can't explain why a wildcat should bite Miss Poore on Vida's behalf, can it?

Do please write to me soon and tell me what I ought to do about informing Miss Annette.

The same to the same:
 I took your advice and told Miss Annette. She said she must trust my discretion not to let the other girls know anything she told me, and then admitted that Vida has been followed by this reputation in every school she's been in, until her father couldn't enter her in some schools. Something unpleasant always happens to any person who displeases Vida di Monserreau. And although she disclaims having done anything, yet she declares it is done for her.
 Miss Annette asked me if I wanted to have my room to myself. I thought that Vida really hadn't done anything to me, and she had certainly made our room the nicest in school. I decided to let her stay on, and Miss Annette thanked me so heartily that I was actually embarrassed.
 . . . Why didn't you tell me Cousin Edgar was coming down? I couldn't imagine who it was when I was called to the reception room to see a gentleman. Imagine my surprise!
 He gave me the chain, mother, and it is perfectly precious! Have you seen it? It's tiny carved cats with their tails in their mouths, and the pendant is a great jade cat with topaz eyes. The girls are wild over it, and Vida particularly is simply crazy about it. She asked me if Cousin Edgar couldn't get her one like it.
 Cousin Edgar said a rather funny thing. He clasped the chain about my neck and declared that I must promise not to take it off without his permission. Now, why do you suppose he did that? When I asked him, he just shrugged his shoulders and said something about your having shown him my letters. What have my letters to do with my promising not to take off the cat-chain?
 Yesterday he came over to take me driving. When he came into the reception room, he thrust out his chin in that odd way of his and said abruptly: 'There's a cat in the room. Thought Miss Annette didn't allow pet animals.'
 I knew there couldn't be one, but he insisted and began to look about the room. And then—the oddest thing, mother! We came upon Vida di Monserreau, asleep in a big armchair

by the fireplace. She had crouched on her knees, with her hands out on the arm of the chair and her chin on her outstretched hands, for all the world like a comfortable pussy-cat.

I said to Cousin Edgar: 'Here's your cat,' and laughed.

He looked at Vida closely. Then he said softly to me, 'Althea, you are speaking more to the point than is your wont.' (You know how he loves to tease me, mother.) 'Introduce me to the pussy,' said he.

I woke Vida. She was terribly embarrassed to have been seen in such an unconventional pose, but she told me afterward that she liked Cousin Edgar more than any other man she'd ever met. I think he liked her, too, although, of course, he didn't say much to me about it.

Vida asked him, almost at once, if he hadn't got another cat-chain like mine. She'd taken a tremendous fancy to it, she said.

'Perhaps you can prevail upon Althea to give you hers. If you can, I'll get her something else to take its place.'

At this suggestion of his, Vida turned imploring eyes upon me. Mother, I was disturbed. I thought of what had happened to Natalie and to Miss Poore, and I wondered if something horrible would happen to me if I refused to give Vida my chain. So I just put it to her point-blank.

'What will happen to me if I don't give my chain to you, Vida?'

'Nothing to you, Althea, darling. I could never be really angry at you,' she whispered.

'Then please don't ask me to give up my chain,' I begged.

I looked back as I went from the room with Cousin Edgar, and her eyes were on me in the most wistful way. Poor Vida!

. . . I wonder what the attraction is? Cousin Edgar is remaining here for an indefinite visit, he says. I do hope he hasn't fallen in love with Alma Henning: I simply cannot bear that girl. I suppose he won't ask my advice, though, if he has fallen in love with one of the girls. Belle Bragg is wild over him, and Natalie thinks him scrumptious.

He has old Peter with him and is stopping at the little hotel in Pine Valley.

The same to the same:
  . . . I suppose I ought to tell you some things I've hardly dared write before because they are so—well, so extraordinary. I've been afraid you might think something the matter with my brain, because I'd been studying too hard. Cousin Edgar says it is in good condition and my head straight on my shoulders, and to write you the whole thing, exactly what I thought about it.

Mother, there *is* something uncanny about Vida di Monserreau. I told you how cat-like she was at times, and how she loves sitting in the dark, or prowling about the room in the dark.

The other day I came into the room ten minutes before lights-out. The room was empty when I turned on the light. But as I went to my desk, a great tortoise-shell cat was stretching itself lazily in the armchair where Vida loves to sit, near the window.

Like a flash Miss Poore's experience passed through my mind and I started for the door. As I got to the hall, I turned around, and—mother, believe me or not—there wasn't a sign of a cat. But sitting in the armchair, staring at me with those queer yellow eyes of hers, was Vida di Monserreau.

I sat down on a chair near the door and breathed hard for a moment. Then I said, 'My gracious, Vida, how you startled me! I didn't see you when I came in. What happened to the cat?'

'Cat?' says she, yawning. 'What cat?' She stretched her arms lazily and settled herself comfortably on the cushions.

I can tell you I felt queer. My eyes had played me a very strange trick, making me see a striped black-and-yellow cat where Vida was sitting. I felt it best to say no more to her for fear she might think me out of my mind. But the more I think about it, the more I am convinced that there was a cat.

And if I did see a cat, stretching and yawning in the

armchair, where, if you please, was Vida when I was looking at the cat? And where did the animal get to? (I looked everywhere before I'd go to bed, although I didn't tell Vida what for. I pretended I'd mislaid my gym. slippers that were all the time in my locker. I could feel her yellow eyes on me while I peeped under the beds and around.)

When I happened to mention the incident to Cousin Edgar, he told me not to forget that I'd promised not to remove the chain he'd given me. He said something about its being a talisman to ward off evil influences.

Now, mother, don't write and tell me not to study so hard! Cousin Edgar doesn't think I'm crazy or delirious, so I guess you needn't.

The same to the same:

... This morning Cousin Edgar called me on the telephone to ask if anything had been stolen from one of the girls last night. There had. Grace Dreene had lost a locket and chain. Cousin Edgar asked if the locket had her initials on it in chip diamonds! How did he know? I'll tell you.

Last night he was sleepless, so he took a walk up here. The moon was shining directly on my side of the dormitory and he distinctly saw a great tortoise-shell cat come out of what he thought was my room.

There is a very narrow ledge around the building, under the windows, about three inches wide. The cat walked along that ledge until it reached Grace's window, where it jumped in. After a moment it came out with something glittering in its mouth!

Cousin Edgar hissed, 'Scat!' The cat hesitated, startled, and the thing went flashing from its mouth to the ground. Cousin Edgar watched it go back to my window, then he picked up the article. It was Grace's locket and chain. The cat had stolen it from Grace's room! Did you ever hear of anything so queer, mother? I've read of monkeys and jackdaws—but a cat!

Cousin Edgar mailed the chain to Grace. Fancy the

astonishment of the girls when the stolen thing came back through the mail!

But what do you make of it? The cat came out of, and went back into my room! The things I do think are so extraordinary that I'm afraid to say them, even to myself.

From Captain Edgar Benedict's notebook:

After having found out all I could from Althea about the strange facts in this most interesting case, I determined to follow the only clue that presented itself, *i.e.*, the old, coloured mammy. It seems that she called regularly every Tuesday, so I made it a point to linger near the academy on a Tuesday morning, and was rewarded by seeing the old woman appear bright and early for her young mistress's laundry.

She is a queer character. Far from being the decrepit old creature I had been led to expect by Althea's description, she is a tall, handsome mulatto woman with flashing eyes that hold a strange magnetism in their direct, unblinking gaze. Her face is deeply lined with wrinkles that to my opinion have been etched by the character of her thoughts rather than by the hand of time. She carries herself humbly when in the presence of academy people, but I have seen her, once out of sight of the school, straighten up that gaunt form and throw her head back proudly, altering her dragging walk into a brisk and lively stride.

She carried the young lady's fresh laundry into the academy and in half an hour came out laden with the soiled laundry, which she had in an embroidered laundry-bag. Once out of the sight of the school, she broke into a rapid, swinging walk, and I had much ado to keep her in sight. She reached Pine Valley and made for the negro quarters, where she entered a house that I noted carefully.

As I wanted very much to get a personal impression, I knocked at her door, and inquired if she could do my laundry work. She stared at me, pride in those black eyes of hers. Then she said very curtly that she did washing for one person only, and shut the door in my face. There is a fierce, implacable atmosphere about that old black woman. I would dislike tremendously to arouse her hatred.

. . . Just got back from a night-visit to Mammy Jinny's cabin. Fortunately, when I got there, she had left a full inch of space between the window-frame and the lower edge of the window-shade. Through it I got a fine view of the old witch—for witch she certainly is, and somehow involved in the mysterious happenings at the academy.

It is not the first time I have watched a witch's incantations. But I have never before had such a strong personal interest in them.

The old negress pulled out the laundry from the bag, and with it tumbled a flashing emerald ring! That must have been the ring of Natalie Cunningham. How did it get into Vida di Monserreau's soiled laundry, unless put there by Vida herself? Is Vida an accomplice or an innocent victim?

Mammy Jinny now drew from her bosom a stocking, and shook out of it as fine a collection of rings, brooches, bracelets, chains, as I've ever seen outside a jeweller's shop. She laid the emerald ring with them and sat staring at her plunder. After a while, she pushed it back into its hiding-place. Then she began to pace the dirt floor of her squalid cabin.

As she walked, she muttered. Sometimes she wrung her hands. Fragments of her words drifted to my ears, as I listened.

'My baby Vida—my little missy! Forgive me, missy! But you must pay for your father's crime. I cannot forgive him!'

All at once she flung herself down before the hearth, for all the world like a great cat and began to stare unblinkingly into the smouldering embers. By my watch, she remained in that posture absolutely motionless for fully two hours, during which I honestly wished I were elsewhere; there was something about her tense attitude that conveyed a baleful significance to my intuition. I knew that she was projecting her mental powers to accomplish her black purposes, like the evil old witch she was. It was hardly an agreeable situation

for me, but I dared not move until she herself began to stir.
I have an idea that the witch, the tortoise-shell cat, and the odd Vida are more closely connected than might seem credible. I must take Althea somewhat into my confidence.

. . . My plan worked perfectly. Vida was very happy to possess the cat-chain and easily agreed not to take it off. Last night I kept watch over the old negress, and Althea—at my request—watched Vida. Vida slept peacefully through the very hours when I watched Mammy Jinny sweating and working her incantations in vain.

. . . I am on the right track. Althea tells me that Mammy Jinny came into the academy and ordered Vida to take off the cat-chain. Vida refused with what seemed natural indignation. Mammy Jinny told her the chain was 'bad voodoo.' Vida stood firm. The old negress was so furious that when she left, she forgot to bow herself, and strode away, full height, much to Vida's astonishment.

. . . Althea has been carrying out my further directions with a cleverness and tact that does her credit. She snipped one of the links in the chain when Vida wasn't looking, and Vida has asked me to have it repaired, as my cousin suggested. Tonight Vida will be without the protection of the chain. I have instructed Althea as to her part, and I shall myself watch the old witch.

. . . All last night Mammy Jinny worked her spells. They were successful this time. Althea has told me what happened.

Althea saw the cat steal from Vida's bed to the window, and return with a stolen bracelet in its mouth. It dropped the article into Vida's laundry-bag. Then, as Althea expressed it, the cat sprang into Vida's bed, and—there lay Vida, peacefully sleeping! No wonder Althea couldn't close her eyes the rest of the night.

When one of the girl's chums came in to say that a bracelet was missing, Althea had it ready to return. She said she had picked it up in the hall.

I am going to put a stop to the whole business. It is voodoo, pure and simple, with a taint of the devil that is unpleasant, to say the least. Whatever the old negress's intentions, she must not attempt to carry them out by means of an innocent young white girl who has somehow fallen under her dominant will-power. If I cannot put a quick stop to it, I shall tell Vida di Monserreau exactly what she has to fear and provide her with a talisman.

Last night was certainly a thrilling one from start to finish. I sent old Peter to remain outside Mammy Jinny's cabin, for I wanted a full report of her actions. I myself, with Miss Annette's kind co-operation, hung a stout rope-ladder from Althea's window while the two inmates of the room were in the gymnasium, and covered the top with pillows to conceal it from prying eyes.

At about one-thirty a.m. the great cat came out of Althea's window—left open for this purpose—and went out upon the narrow ledge. It made me hold my breath. (What if it had fallen? The thought makes me shudder yet.) It disappeared within another open window, and I went quickly under the window and called to Althea that it was the fifth window. She closed hers at once and went to Belle Bragg's room, where the cat had gone in.

Both girls saw it go out of the window. Then Belle looked at her dressing-table and found her wrist-watch missing. Althea said she thought one of the girls had borrowed it and would bring it back in the morning. Then Belle closed her window—a vain precaution—and Althea returned to her own room.

Meantime, I had mounted the ladder quietly until I was directly under Althea's window, where I braced myself strongly for what I had in mind would follow.

The cat found the window closed. It beat with its fore-paws at the pane in a pitiful manner.

I reached up and tossed the repaired cat-chain about its neck. Although I had rather anticipated what followed, it made me gasp, for it was the limp, unconscious body of Vida di Monserreau that I supported in my arms!

Althea opened the window and between us we got the

poor girl on to her bed. I warned Althea to be silent, and was off to find old Peter and get his report.

I was thoroughly provoked when I found he was not on watch outside the cabin as I had expected him to be. Then I peered under the window-shade. What I saw was my old black Peter, squatting on the floor before the hearth, his arm about that old witch and her head resting on his shoulder!

I *was* furious! I gave a thundering rap at the door. Peter let me in. But the old scoundrel, instead of seeming ashamed and guilty, met me with a broad grin that showed his white teeth from ear to ear. To my further astonishment, Mammy Jinny rose to her full height with a grin that matched his.

It took my breath away. I demanded an explanation. Between them, it was mighty hard to find out the truth, for it was a long story that went back to the young girlhood of the old negress.

She and Peter were slaves, owned by Vida's grandfather. When a valuable ring was missing, the old man charged Peter with the theft, and sold him into a distant state where he could never hope to see his wife again. Jinny knew the facts but what good would it have done her to have told them? She might have received a whipping. She knew that her young master had given the ring to a white girl whom he was courting on the sly.

Jinny appealed to 'young marse'. He laughed in her face. She determined then to be revenged. Concealing her hatred, she demanded and received the care of Vida, when 'young marse's' wife died in child-birth.

From that time on, Mammy Jinny worked out her plans, using her knowledge of voodoo, until she had so bent the child's will to hers that Vida was absolutely responsive to the old negress's thoughts. How she performed the apparent metamorphosis I had seen, she would not tell, however, but only looked at me defiantly out of her proud eyes.

Mammy's idea of revenge seems to have been to fasten the disgrace of theft upon Vida di Monserreau thus shaming 'young marse'. Her methods of accomplishing her end are, like all methods of black magic, better left undisclosed to the general public.

As old Peter has long owed me loyalty, since I saved his life years ago, I had little difficulty in persuading him to take his wife to Jamaica, from which place they were originally bought, and where Peter in later years returned, in hope of meeting Jinny there once more. They will be out of Vida's life henceforth.

This does not mean that Vida is to go unprotected. I shall take care of that, with the permission of her father. But I do not believe that old Jinny will ever again crouch in invocation to the Evil Powers to bring the tortoise-shell cat into materialisation at Vida's expense.

The Looking-Glass Tree

JOAN AIKEN

Both a cat and magic feature again in this next story by Joan Aiken, but the feline is a family pet whose shape is forcibly changed and the magic is of a rather different kind to that which we have just read about. When Walrus, the large, fat cat which belongs to Mark and Harriet Armitage is turned into a wolf by the children's strange new neighbour, they seek the aid of a conjuror who is travelling with a fair that has just arrived in the village to restore him to his original form. And that proves to be their passport into a whole new dimension of the supernatural. Joan Aiken, who is one of the best modern fantasy writers, has a special insight into the minds of children and the supernormal, too, and displays this talent to considerable effect in "The Looking-Glass Tree". I am particularly pleased to be publishing this story here for the first time, and by the fact that we shall be meeting another member of the gifted Aiken family later in the collection.

They were putting up the village fair on the green. It was a long job. The thud-thud of hammers banging in the posts for coconut-shies echoed all over the village, along with the cheerful stutter of generating motors hoisting the big roundabout into position. The village green was on quite a steep slope, and the big roundabout had to be propped under its lower side on piles of bricks, an arrangement which Mr Armitage condemned as crazily unsafe. Each year he earnestly begged his children not to ride on the roundabout. Each year they pointed out that the fair had been going since 1215 with no particular loss of life. Otherwise they took no notice of his warnings.

Mr Armitage sat in his downstairs study, trying to work, but the noise distracted him, which was a pity, as he had the house to himself for once. Mrs Armitage was out for the day visiting a sick cousin, Mark and Harriet were down on the green, watching the fair put itself together.

'During the last year sugar prices have declined rapidly,' wrote Mr Armitage, trying to ignore the sound of thumping. Then he realised that what he heard was not the distant hammering, but somebody banging on his window. He looked up from the report on sugar he was trying to write, and found himself staring into the unattractive face of Miss Pursey.

Miss Pursey had bought the small field next to the Armitage garden six months ago. Nobody quite knew how this had happened, as old Mr Fewkes who previously owned the field had often said he would never sell it, and if he did so, he would sell it to the Armitages. But then, suddenly one day, he *had* sold it. 'I dunno what came over me,' he said helplessly to Mr Armitage in the pub, 'seemed as 'ow the young lady 'ad an uncommon argymentative persuading way o' going on at me.' And in less than a week after that a firm of builders unfamiliar to the Armitages had begun slapping up a bungalow, and in a suspiciously short time after *that*, not more than a month, all was completed, and Miss Pursey moved into her house.

It seemed almost certain that Miss Pursey was a witch. The bungalow, although made from pre-cast concrete, was constructed so as to resemble a witch's cottage, with a roof made from sections of plastic thatch, fake diamond-paning in the windows, and Tudor beams painted on the walls.

'She has roses and hollyhocks painted growing up the walls, too,' reported Harriet who had been over to watch the builders in action. 'Even the bees were fooled.'

The back of the bungalow, in complete contrast, was painted with a *trompe-l'oeil* reproduction of a Greek temple, done in such ingenious, deceitful perspective that it was good enough to fool anyone, not only bees, until they were about two feet away; one or two of Mr Fewkes's sheep who wandered into the field through a gap in the hedge were seen trying to push their way among the painted Doric columns and looking as puzzled as only sheep can look because they were unable to do so.

But Miss Pursey, when she moved in, soon discouraged the sheep. In no time at all she had a boring, tidy garden laid out, a lot of square beds neatly dug, divided by cinder paths.

'She waters her plants with boiling water,' Harriet reported.

She also watered the sheep with boiling water, until they took the hint and retired to their own side of the hedge.

Miss Pursey was not neighbourly. She had such a very discouraging expression on her face while she dug her beds and marked off her seed-drills that the Armitages, without even discussing the matter, left her strictly alone.

Mr Armitage was therefore surprised, and not best pleased, to find her banging on his study window at eleven o'clock on a Monday morning.

Miss Pursey was tall, plump, and brisk in her movements. She was not old—in her mid-twenties perhaps—but extremely plain. She wore her straight black hair in a bun at the back and cut in a no-nonsense fringe at the front. She also wore a mini-skirt, which was a mistake, as it left bare most of two large, bulging legs tapering down to small stubby feet in spike-heeled shoes; the legs looked like two exclamation points: !! supporting a capital O. She had very large black-rimmed glasses—two more O's—through which she directed an accusing glare at Mr Armitage as he reluctantly opened the window. He thought that if she had not so obviously been a witch she might have been a gym-instructor or hockey teacher.

'Your cat—' said Miss Pursey angrily as soon as he had the catch undone.

'How do you do,' said Mr Armitage with great politeness, opening the window to its full extent. 'I believe we have not formally introduced ourselves yet. I am Everard Gilbert Armitage—delighted to meet you, Miss—er?'

'Pearl Pursey,' she said snappishly. 'Your cat, Mr Armitage, is wrecking my tree.'

She turned and pointed.

Mr Armitage, unwillingly stepping out through the window (which was a French one) followed her to the wicket gate in the boundary hedge which separated the Armitage garden from Miss Pursey's field.

Just beyond the hedge a small tree was growing. And in the branches of the tree, looking very unsuitable—for he was about half its size—but very pleased with himself, was the Armitages' enormously large black cat Walrus, so called because he wore his top front teeth outside his chin, like a walrus's tusks. The teeth were sticking out now even more than usual, as he dangled self-consciously over two branches of the tiny tree, making it sway about like a fishing-rod with a polar bear balanced on top of it.

Mr Armitage immediately thought of two things.

He remembered that the tree had been growing there before Miss Pursey arrived, so that in a way it could not be said to be her tree; she certainly had not planted it.

He also remembered that the strip of land immediately beyond the Armitage boundary hedge was in fact a footpath; a right of way leading across the fields to the next village. Nobody used it any more, because it was more comfortable to go round by road, which was why the little tree had had a chance to grow up. But actually neither the tree, nor the land it grew on, belonged to Miss Pursey; they were public property.

However Mr Armitage didn't believe in crossing his bridges before they were built, preferred peace and quiet, and wanted to get on with his report about sugar. He did not mention any of these things but merely remarked,

'A cat, ma'am, in law, is counted as a member of the class *ferae naturae* for whose actions the owners cannot be held responsible.'

'I don't care a twopenny fig for your idiotic law,' snapped Miss Pursey. 'I want that cat removed before it does irreparable damage to my tree.' And she glared at Walrus, who swayed serenely about in the branches of the tiny tree with his tail stuck out sideways to avoid getting it entangled in a twig.

Mr Armitage said, 'Here, puss, puss!' wondering as he did so why Miss Pursey did not herself remove the cat. He was well within reach, for the tree was only four feet high.

Walrus took no notice of Mr Armitage.

'I'll have to go back to the house and bang on his plate,' Mr Armitage said, and did so. Walrus ate his meals off a tin plate the sound of which, when banged with a spoon, always fetched him at a gallop, no matter how far off he was. It was the only time he did gallop. As soon as he heard the banging now, he dropped from the tree like a sack of coal, leaving it wildly swaying, and shot off to the kitchen, where Mr Armitage had to open a tin of sardines, as there seemed to be no cat-food.

'And don't go up that tree any more,' he admonished Walrus, who took no notice. He was busy flicking sardine-oil about with his whiskers.

Miss Pursey did not thank Mr Armitage. She was to be seen in the distance, angrily inspecting the little tree for damage.

Mr Armitage shut his study window and went back to work.

But at lunch (a cold one assembled by the children from ingredients left by Mrs Armitage) there came a furious rapping at the garden door.

'Your cat,' said Miss Pursey to Harriet, who opened the door, 'is up my tree *again*. Please come and remove it at once.'

Harriet went through the gate in the hedge and lifted Walrus out of the tree. He allowed himself to be lifted, but he looked martyred about it and let his back legs dangle down, always a sign that he was not pleased. 'You see he remembers that there used to be a chaffinch's nest in the hedge beside that tree,' Harriet explained.

'I don't care what kind of a nest there was, or what he remembers,' Miss Pursey said. 'Don't let this happen again, or I shall be obliged to take drastic action.'

'My goodness!' Harriet said, returning to the lunch-table. 'Miss Pursey's got some really awful-looking plaster gnomes in her garden, wheeling little barrows full of skulls. They're enough to give anyone nightmares.'

'And did you notice the plastic toadstools?' said her father.

'The red-and-white spotted ones?' said Harriet. 'Those aren't plastic. I had a good look at them. They're real. She must have been sowing quick-grow-toadstool spores. I've read about those red-and-white ones. On the Steppes of Siberia they are regarded as a great delicacy and may be sold for three or four reindeer apiece.'

'Well we are not in Siberia now,' said her father, 'and have no reindeer, thank heaven. Don't eat any of those toadstools; they give you hallucinations.'

'I suppose the Siberians like hallucinations,' Mark said thoughtfully.

In the next few days a great many more toadstools and fungi sprouted in Miss Pursey's garden, including *Amanita Phalloides*, the Death Cap, which gives anybody who eats it three or four days of increasingly unpleasant sensations, ending in death. Miss Pursey had a whole bed full of Death Caps. She had also Stink Horns, False Blushers, Sickeners, Devil's Boletus, and Lurid Boletus. As well as her fungi she had several handsome bushes of Deadly Nightshade covered with large glossy black fruits—enough, as Mr Armitage said, regarding them apprehensively, to poison the whole village. He strongly recommended his children to keep well away from Miss Pursey's garden.

'But we have to keep going in to get Walrus out of the tree,' objected Mark.

Walrus, not an intelligent cat, seemed obsessed by memories of the chaffinch's nest. He spent as much of his time as possible in the little tree, which was developing a permanent list towards the hedge. Mark and Harriet had to make constant rescue dashes, and Harriet worried about the situation. They could not keep guard over Walrus for twenty-four hours a day—after all they had to go to school—and it seemed likely that any drastic action taken by Miss Pursey would be very drastic indeed.

'I wonder why she doesn't take Walrus out of the tree herself?' said Mark.

'I expect it's because cats are witch-animals,' suggested Harriet. 'Probably you aren't allowed to touch somebody else's familiar.'

'But Walrus isn't anyone's familiar.'

'I know, but *she* doesn't know that.'

'She could do something at long-distance—lasso him or shoot him.'

'Don't!' shuddered Harriet.

Familiar or unfamiliar, one evening Walrus did not arrive at his usual headlong speed when Harriet banged the tin-plate supper gong.

There followed a long, worried wait.

'Oh goodness,' said Harriet with quivering lip, 'I do hope Miss Pursey hasn't done something awful. Do you think we should go round and ask—'

'Half a mo,' said Mark. 'Something's trying to get through the cat-flap.'

Something was having a hard struggle.

'*Oh!*' cried Harriet, 'if that fiend has hurt Walrus—'

She rushed to the door and opened it. At once it was plain why the creature outside had been unable to get in through the cat-flap. A fullgrown timber wolf bounded past Harriet into the kitchen. He stood about three foot high, weighed two hundred and fifty pounds, and was covered in a thick shaggy greyish-white coat with a splendid ruff round his neck.

Mark and Harriet were disconcerted but the wolf seemed quite accustomed to his surroundings; he made straight for Walrus's tin plate and sucked up the small portion of chopped rock-salmon that lay on it with one scoop of his long supple tongue. Then he looked round for more.

'Oh gosh,' said Harriet, 'has she changed Walrus to this?'

'Looks like it,' said Mark. He approached the wolf with caution and felt under the silvery sweep of ruff. 'Yes! Here's

Walrus's flea-collar—lucky for him it was the stretch kind.'

'It must be stretched pretty far. Do you think it's too tight for him?'

'Seems okay. We'd better leave it on; I daresay wolves have fleas too.'

Wolf-Walrus quite plainly thought one small portion of fish wholly insufficient and demanded more with a long lugubrious howl.

'All right—here—' said Harriet, hastily dumping out the rest of the panful. 'I'm afraid he's going to be expensive to feed—almost as bad as darling Furry.'

Furry had been a griffin who lodged briefly with the Armitages and who required at least forty bowls of bread and milk a day, with raisins.

'Very handsome, though,' said Mark, admiringly stroking the muscular shoulders with their tremendous coat of fur, as Wolf snuffled down the rest of the fish. 'I quite like the idea of having a wolf.'

Mrs Armitage did not like it when she came into the kitchen to make supper.

'Children! What *have* you got there?'

Wolf, stretched in front of the stove, took up the entire hearth-rug.

'Miss Pursey has turned Walrus into a wolf. We'll have to enlarge the cat-flap quite a lot,' Harriet said. 'But don't worry—Mark can do it with his fretsaw. I don't know if Wolf will be able to squeeze through the bathroom window, though.'

Wolf had a try. It was plain that he had not yet grown accustomed to the change in his size. At two in the morning the Armitages woke to a rending crash, and soon after, Mark was almost suffocated by Wolf's two hundred and fifty pounds spread out on top of his eiderdown. Next day it was discovered that the bathroom window-frame had been stove in.

And the carpets and table-legs soon began to suffer severely.

'I really don't think we can keep him,' Mrs Armitage said. 'Besides, he's much more short-tempered than he used to be. Walrus was always such a placid cat. Perhaps some zoo—'

'Oh, Mother! How *could* you? Why, it's our old *Walrus*, that we've had ever since he was a kitten—'

'Well, you'll have to approach Miss Pursey. Ask her to change him back. But be tactful—I don't want you changed to owls or weasels—'

'You'd think Miss Pursey might be glad to change him back, actually,' said Harriet. 'He does quite as much damage in his wolf-shape.'

Certainly Walrus no longer tried to climb the little tree. Timber wolves do not climb trees; which was just as well, for two hundred and fifty pounds of Wolf-Walrus would have done for the tree completely. But wolves dig a lot; and Miss Pursey was often to be seen throwing furious stones after Walrus who had just scooped out a large cavity in her hemlock-bed or among her poison-ivy.

Mark went round to the bungalow, as he had not yet come into conflict with Miss Pursey, and put the case to her politely.

'I expect he's got over his tree-habit by now—Walrus has a very short memory. He's quite a stupid cat. Couldn't you see your way to change him back?'

But Miss Pursey was unapproachable.

'Why should I?' she snapped. 'I have just about lost my patience with your family. You give me nothing but trouble. Get out of my garden and don't let me see you in it again.'

Mark left before she lost any more patience.

'We'll have to think of something else,' he said to Harriet.

'I've had an idea,' she said. 'There's a new stall at the Fair, this year, Janie Perrow was telling me—it's a magician. Janie says he's marvellous. He can cure all sorts of illnesses and change spring onions into diamonds—I bet he could change a wolf back into a cat. Though it does seem rather a pity,' she added, wrapping an arm round Walrus's huge grey bulk. He snapped at her hand in his sleep. They were sitting on the hearth-rug after tea.

'Let's go down to the fair now,' said Mark, jumping up. 'Have you any money?'

'A pound, saved from hop-picking.'

'I've got two. Perhaps Father will give us something. A magician might be expensive.'

Mr Armitage was cautious. 'First find out if the chap will do it. Then find out how much it costs. Then I'll see.' He added gloomily, 'it would be more useful if he could find some way of removing Miss Pursey. However, do your best.'

Mark and Harriet ran down to the fair which was spread all over the village green.

It was called the Sloe-Fair, happened once a year, and lasted for two weeks, from six to midnight every night. The stalls and sideshows were all terribly expensive, so Mark and Harriet usually waited and went on the last night, which was always the gayest and wildest, when pigs and coconuts and goldfish were being auctioned off, and the fair-people, having made a good deal of money, were more inclined to let customers on to the swings and roundabouts at half-price, if half-price was all they could afford, rather than let them go home with any money left unspent.

The roundabout, perched slantways on the hillside, was a particularly good one, with dragons and cockatrices, griffins, unicorns, hydras, cameleopards and Tasmanian Devils, all painted in brilliant and luminous colours. It made a tremendous noise of bawling music and grinding machinery. Mark and Harriet each had one ride on it before getting down to business with the magician; he chose a dragon and she a cockatrice. It really felt like flying as one swung out over the tremendous drop on the lower side.

Close by the roundabout stood a very small stall indeed. It was hardly larger than a horse-box and had a sign on top, very brightly painted, illuminated by light-bulbs all round, which said, MAESTRO CAPPODOCCIO, Leech to the Old Man of the Mountains, Tooth-Puller to Prester John,

Chirurgeon to the Grand Lama, Hakim to the Bey of Tunis. And his Superb Assistant Alicia Morgiana, Queen of the Sorceresses. Not to mention Lupus, the Wisest Beast in Christendom.

'This must be our man,' said Mark. 'There doesn't seem to be much going on in his van, though.'

Indeed the little van, which was on wheels, seemed dark and silent enough. The door was closed. A small window on one side gave out a dim gleam of light.

Harriet stood on tiptoe and peered through the window. 'I can see someone in there sitting on a stool,' she reported. So she went round to the end, climbed up the two steps, and tapped on the door. After a considerable pause it was slowly pulled back.

Inside stood a pale girl with lanky fair hair and a good many spots. She wore a sagging skirt, a bedraggled cardigan, trodden-over shoes, and a lot of mascara. She was chewing gum. She hardly looked like the Queen of the Sorceresses.

'Is Maestro Cappodoccio about?' asked Harriet.

'I couldn't say, I'm sure,' said the girl, as if she didn't care, either. She had a flat, uninterested voice.

'When will he be back?'

'I couldn't say. He'll be back some time.'

'Are you his assistant?'

'Yes,' the girl said, shifting her gum from one cheek to the other.

'Well can you help us?'

'Nah. Not without the Professor.'

'Well can we come in and wait?'

'Suppose so,' said the girl unenthusiastically, and went back to her stool. They edged inside. The van was about five foot by seven—large enough to accommodate four or five people standing but not much more. At the far end was a stove, with a black pot boiling. The walls were lined with shelves containing small pots and jars labelled Ac. Phen., Ol. Euc., Sod. Bic., etc. There were two pull-down bunks. The ceiling was painted with geometrical signs. The girl's stool was the only seat, and she had gone back to reading GIRL'S STAR WEEKLY.

Mark and Harriet each stood facing a wall. Harriet's had the window in it; she discovered with surprise that it was not a window but a picture. One-way glass, perhaps? It had certainly been a window from the outside. But now, instead of the fairground, she saw, very far away, a garden with mossy lawns, weeping willows, a fountain, a stone seat—

'Gosh,' murmured Harriet, half to herself. 'It isn't a picture. It's real.' She had noticed that the weeping willow was swaying in the breeze.

She jogged Mark's elbow.

'Hey—look at this. It's a real garden—miles and miles away—'

'Sure it's not a TV screen?' murmured Mark, turning round cautiously so as not to knock any of the little pots. But as soon as he studied the framed garden he went very pale—his eyes almost popped out of his head. '*Harriet!* Do you know what that is?'

'No, what?' She glanced warningly at the girl, but the girl was absorbed in an article about Your Stars, Your Make-Up, and You.

'That garden!' hissed Mark. 'It's Mr Johansen's garden. Wait here! I'm going to fetch him right away!'

And without wasting a moment he slipped out of the van and rushed off into the dusk.

Harriet had known immediately what he meant. Mark's music-teacher, a kind, sad, white-haired man called Rudolph Johansen had once, many years ago, fallen in love with a German princess whom he had the misfortune to lose through a piece of drawing-room magic. Somewhere, folded up in an enchanted garden inside the pages of a book, the Princess Sophia Maria Luisa of Saxe-Hoffenpoffen-und-Hamster was still waiting for Mr Johansen, but nobody knew where she was or where the book was. It had been lost. But now here, according to Mark, was a picture of her garden—no, the garden itself, Harriet thought—and Mark should know, for

THE LOOKING-GLASS TREE

he had once cut it all carefully off the sides of six cereal packets and pasted it together, only to have it destroyed during some disastrous spring-cleaning.

Harriet gazed at the garden as if it might melt away in front of her eyes.

Far in the distance she saw a speck of silvery white, which slowly came closer and turned into a tiny, faraway lady, stiffly dressed in a white crinoline, with her powdered hair dragged high on top of her head. Miles away, at the far end of the lawn, she sat herself rather wearily down on a stone seat, laying her hand on the head of a big shaggy dog who sat down on the ground by her feet.

'That must be Princess Sophie!' Harriet thought. 'If only Mark can find Mr Johansen—and if only Mr Johansen can remember his tune—' For entry to the garden could only be achieved by humming a tune which Mr Johansen himself had made up.

'Hey,' said Alicia the Queen of the Sorceresses, closing her magazine and standing up. 'I can hear the Professor coming, and he's got someone with him. Only one customer allowed at a time. You'd best wait outside.'

'But we were here first,' Harriet protested.

'Can't help that,' said the girl, and jerked her head towards the door.

Harriet went out and stood beside the van, in its shadow. She could hear voices and footsteps approaching, for the merry-go-round was temporarily at a standstill. Then, at her feet, she heard the rattle of a chain.

Rather startled she looked down and saw a large paw extending from under the van.

It looked suspiciously like that of Walrus.

Harriet dropped on her knees. Her eyes were accustomed to the dim light; she found herself staring straight into the face of a large pale-grey wolf.

Was it Walrus?

Very cautiously she held out a hand. 'Are you Walrus?' she whispered.

A low growl answered her.

The voices and footsteps had now arrived outside the van.

Harriet heard a man's voice—a dry, gentle, calm voice, rather like that of Mr Garrett, her English master, who liked to recite such long poems that not infrequently he put the whole class to sleep.

'But, madam, I already *have* a wolf in my act,' he was saying. 'As you can see from my sign. I have Lupus, the Wisest Beast in Christendom, who can tell gold from sham by touch and recognises all the letters of the Greek alphabet.'

'That's why I thought you'd like to have two.' The other voice was Miss Pursey's—Harriet recognised it at once. 'Two would be better still. You could teach the second one the Russian alphabet—it's a Siberian wolf, actually—and how to tell butter from marge.'

'Why do you wish to dispose of the animal?'

'It's a nuisance in the garden,' said Miss Pursey.

Harriet's blood boiled. Oh, the monster! she thought. Not content with turning our poor Walrus into a wolf, she's now arranging to sell him into captivity.

'I'd have to see the animal before I could come to a decision,' the man—presumably Maestro Cappodoccio—said. 'If you like to bring him here I'll give you my answer.'

'Oh, very well,' said Miss Pursey annoyedly, and her steps receded into the dark again.

The magician went into his van. Harriet followed him at once.

'That woman who just offered you a wolf,' she began in high indignation. 'She's no right to! For a start, it isn't a wolf at all, but our cat Walrus! And—'

Professor Cappodoccio looked at Harriet attentively. He was a plump, grey-haired man with kind, but very compelling brown eyes. She had interrupted him in the act of putting on a black robe over his ordinary grey suit.

'You say the animal is not a wolf—' he began.

At that moment Mark and Mr Johansen arrived with most unceremonious speed.

'May we come in, sir?' gasped Mark, and instantly did so. He was dragging Mr Johansen by the arm. Both of them were out of breath. 'Look!' panted Mark triumphantly to his music-teacher. 'Look—there she is!'

He pointed jerkily to the tiny telescoped garden where the ant-sized Princess Sophie was thoughtfully pulling her large dog's ears.

'Ach!' breathed Mr Johansen joyfully. 'Ach, yes! Zat is my Sophie! Ach, Himmel, I never zsought to zsee her more!' He was terribly moved. Tears stood in his eyes. His chest, which was still heaving from the speed of their run, began to heave also with suppressed sobs.

'Can you call out to her, sir?' gulped Mark. 'Attract her attention?'

Mr Johansen shook his head. He was still too out of breath for that. But he handed Mark a tiny silver dog-whistle. Mark, still very puffed, blew one short soft note on the whistle. It was quick, but it was enough for the dog in the garden to catch it. Up shot her head—and suddenly she was off at a gallop, careering like the wind along the length of the huge lawn. It was plain that she was barking in wild delight, but she was still so far away that no sound could be heard, until she reached the very edge of the frame, when, faintly, faintly, they could hear a faraway reverberation of tiny barks. She was running this way and that, obviously much puzzled.

And the princess, equally startled, had risen to her feet—was apparently calling to the dog—asking what was the matter.

'Am I to understand, sir,' inquired Professor Cappodoccio with sympathetic interest, 'that you are acquainted with the lady and the dog in my wall-hanging? I have long wondered—'

'Ach, szo! Zat is no wall-hanging—zat is ze garten of Princess Sophia of Saxe-Hoffenpoffen. *Indeed* I am acqvainted wizz it! In one little minute I sing a song wvich—'

But in one little minute a whole lot of other things happened, very unexpectedly. Miss Pursey reappeared, looking decidedly ruffled, with a set of parallel scratches on her face; she held both ends of a rope which she had passed under the collar of an equally angry-looking Walrus. Apparently once he had lost his cat-form she had more control of him.

Observing that there were several people in the van—though the only one she could see from the steps was Mr Johansen—Miss Pursey tied Walrus's rope to the door handle, and called out,

'Dr Cappodoccio! Can you come out here a moment?'

At the sound of her loud, peremptory voice Dr Cappodoccio's assistant, the pale bored Alicia, reacted with startling speed. She leapt to her feet, dropping the GIRL'S STAR WEEKLY, and darted to the doorway, moving through the group of people as fast as an adder shooting through a patch of dry grass. And her whole appearance changed; the look of languid discontent dropped away, replaced by malevolent purposefulness.

'Well, there!' she exclaimed triumphantly. 'I didn't *think* I could mistake that voice! If it isn't our Playful Pearl, the pride of Beelzebub Training College! Dear old pushy Pearl, the most unpopular girl on the necromantic campus—Pal Pearl, who wouldn't ever *dream* of cribbing another student's incantation, or pinching someone else's spell-tables, or borrowing their six-pointed star-calculator and forgetting to return it, oh, *no*!'

She shot her face forward to within an inch of Miss Pursey, who looked somewhat discomposed.

'What about my pyramid that you stole just before final examinations? What did you do with it?' hissed Alicia.

'Pyramid? What pyramid?' riposted Pursey loftily. 'My good girl, I haven't the least idea what you are maundering on about. Just because you did badly in your finals is no excuse for trying to put the blame on others—it's not my fault if you came bottom.'

'No? I've come on quite a bit since then, though,' said Alicia with menace, and she pointed her pale skinny finger at Miss Pursey. A blue flash wriggled along it, and suddenly a blaze of cobalt fire enveloped Miss Pursey, who emerged from it quite bald, and very angry indeed. Her spectacles had melted in the heat and fallen off. She glared at Alicia shortsightedly and extended all her fingers, which spurted white fire.

'Hussy!'
'Jade!'
'Minx!'
'Doxy!'
'Strumpet!'

They lunged at each other, feinting and sidestepping like fencers. Alicia's cardigan burst into flame and she tossed it off. A black bat, dislodged from Miss Pursey's handbag, fluttered off with indignant high-pitched squeaks. Absorbed in their dispute the two sorceresses, flaming, sparking, making serpentine darts at each other, kept moving towards the big roundabout, which was now whirling round again, high above them, with its tremendous music, noise, and light.

Harriet watched riveted with suspense as the pair, slashing at each other with their white and blue fire, shouting inaudible insults at one another, edged closer and closer under the side of the roundabout. And then finally there came a prodigious blinding flash and a crash; the whole merry-go-round keeled over—amid bangs, bumps, sounds of splitting wood and shrieks of consternation.

Mark, Dr Cappodoccio and Mr Johansen dashed out of the van; people came rushing from all over the fairground.

And just to add to the general hurly-burly, Walrus and Dr Cappodoccio's wolf Lupus had discovered one another and were at each other's throats in a second, snarling, biting, and rolling over and over.

'Walrus! Stop that at *once*! I'm *surprised* at you!' exclaimed Harriet, and dragged him away from Lupus, getting considerably scratched in the process. She shut him in the van.

Mark and the two men had rushed to the scene of the

accident and she joined them. Already ambulances, police-cars, fire-engines, and breakdown trucks were converging from all sides.

Luckily, though there were plenty of black eyes, scrapes, and bruises, nobody seemed to be seriously hurt. The injured were given first aid and allowed to go. But, oddly enough, there seemed to be no trace of either Miss Pursey or Alicia.

When all was quiet again Harriet, Mark, and Mr Johansen returned to the magician's van.

The little garden scene was still quietly there on the wall, as if none of this tremendous excitement had been taking place outside. But the Princess Sophie and the dog Lotta were gone. The garden was empty. The only intimation that any dog had been present was Walrus on the floor below, restored to cat form, hissing angrily, with his tail swelled up like a chimney-sweep's brush, as it did when he met any dog.

'I sing ze song,' said Mr Johansen. 'Zey wvill come back, I hope.'

Trembling a little, very carefully, he hummed his tune.

But nothing happened. Nobody came. The garden stayed the same size.

Mr Johansen sang the song again. Still nothing happened.

'I'm afraid,' said Dr Cappodoccio compassionately, 'all that black magic going on outside must have left a concentration of poison in the atmosphere and some destructive vibrations, which have upset your spell. *What* a pity.'

'Oh, curse that Miss Pursey!' said Mark furiously. 'It's all her fault. I hope the roundabout squashed her flat.'

'*Poor* Mr Johansen,' said Harriet.

Mr Johansen looked so utterly white, tired, and defeated that Dr Cappodoccio, evidently a kind-hearted man, suggested,

'Why don't you spend the night with me, sir? You can have my assistant's bunk (a most disagreeable, unhelpful girl; I am not at all sorry that she has gone). By tomorrow when the vibrations have settled, perhaps your spell will work once more.'

Mr Johansen allowed himself to be persuaded. Mark and Harriet went rather dismally home, taking it in turns to carry Walrus, who was still uttering frightful threats against the Wisest Wolf in Christendom.

'I've never known him so aggressive,' Harriet remarked.

'The whole evening was a mess,' Mark muttered bitterly as they went up to bed.

However the next morning showed that the evening had not been a total disaster.

It was plain that Miss Pursey had never come home, and in her absence her house was rapidly collapsing, melting, decaying and sinking into the ground, like a very old mushroom. Already most of it was gone. Many of the plants in her garden had died; the only thing that still seemed living and healthy was the little tree on the footpath.

And Walrus, after all, was once more their old familiar outsize monster of a fat black cat.

'Though in a way we shall rather miss having a wolf,' Harriet said, hugging him. Walrus turned and bit her, quite hard. She gazed at him in astonished reproach.

Halfway through the morning Dr Cappodoccio's van drew up outside the front door. Mr Johansen climbed out of it and rang the front-door bell.

'Hasn't the spell worked yet, Mr Johansen?' Harriet asked him anxiously, as she opened the door.

'Ach, no! Not yet!' he sighed. 'And zso ziss Dr Cappodoccio has very kindly inwited me to go wizz him on his woyages and be his assistant. Zen, wven ze spell comes out clear once more, I wvill be on ze spot.'

'Oh dear,' Mark said sadly. 'We shall miss you, Mr Johansen!'

'Shall you know *how* to be a magician's assistant?' Harriet asked doubtfully.

'He wvill teach me; is not difficult, he tell me.'

'You'll find it a bit different from giving piano lessons.'

Mark and Harriet accompanied Mr Johansen to the gate; both were rather dismayed at the thought of the gentle old man abandoning his house and gipsying off in this unexpected manner.

Dr Cappodoccio had left the van, and was standing by their garden hedge, gazing at the little tree that Miss Pursey had been so keen to protect.

He seemed quite excited about it.

'Do you know that you have a great treasure here?' he said, his brown eyes shining with enthusiasm. 'In three years' time that will be a full-grown Looking-Glass Tree.'

'What's a Looking-Glass Tree?' asked Harriet.

'Oh, my dear young lady! The Looking-Glass Tree is the ninth wonder of the world! It grows but once in a hundred years, takes four years to come to full growth, is found only on waste or common land, has leaves that reflect the sun in unrivalled splendour, flowers of incomparable beauty, fruits that will cure any disease from Bell's Palsy to Housemaid's Knee; its bark is unequalled as an ingredient for distilling spells, potions, simples, and compounds. It breathes out a scent that cures deafness and phlebitis for eighty miles around—'

'Really?' said Mark, turning to look at the humble little tree; it might have been an apple or a quince; it seemed to have nothing particularly special about it.

'So *that* was why Miss Pursey bought this bit of land!'

'But if the tree can do all these things in three years' time —will it be able to help Mr Johansen find his princess?'

'Dear me yes! One leaf—a *third* of a leaf—will give anyone the thing he loves most.'

'What a shame that it can't do it *now*!'

'Never mind—in zsree years' time we come back,' said Mr Johansen with his gentle smile, and the two old gentlemen got into their gaily-painted van and drove off, with Lupus the wise wolf sitting between them. Dr Cappodoccio turned his head to shout,

'Mind you look after the tree!'

'It's going to be a bit of a responsibility,' sighed Harriet.

Miss Pursey never reappeared. Strangely enough, two skeletons were found under the wreckage of the roundabout. But they could not have been those of Miss Pursey and Alicia Queen of the Sorceresses, for they were many thousands of years old; local archaeologists became quite excited about them.

Mr Armitage said: 'I *told* you that roundabout was unsafe. I always said so.'

The fat cat Walrus was never so placid again. Into extreme old age he retained several regrettable habits that he had acquired during the time that he was a wolf.

The Human Angle

WILLIAM TENN

After ghosts, the vampire is perhaps the best known denizen of darkness, an undead being that walks only by night and must return to its grave before the first rays of morning sunshine break over the horizon. The vampire needs human blood to preserve its 'existence' according to folk lore, and while stories of these creatures are to be found in abundance in Europe (the most famous vampire of them all, Bram Stoker's Count Dracula, is, of course, based on Transylvanian legends and the life of a fifteenth century Rumanian prince, Vlad Dracul, renowned for his terrible cruelty), they are not entirely unknown in Britain and America. The vampire has to seize its victim at night and draw the life-blood by biting the unfortunate person on the neck—a scene vividly portrayed in many stories and an unending series of films. Among such a vast amount of material, it is a delight to find a story on the vampire theme as unusual as "The Human Angle" which comes from the talented and imaginative William Tenn. It is also one of the very few such stories to feature a child in a central role.

What a road! What filthy, dismal, blinding rain! And, by the ghost of old Horace Greeley, what an idiotic, impossible assignment!

John Shellinger cursed the steamy windscreen from which a monotonous wiper flipped raindrops. He stared through the dripping, half-clear triangle of glass and tried to guess which was broken country road and which was the overgrown brown vegetation of autumn. He might have passed the slowly moving line of murderous men stretching to right and left across country and road; he might have angled off into a side-road and be heading off into completely forsaken land. But he didn't think he had.

What an assignment!

'Get the human angle on this vampire hunt,' Randall had ordered. 'All the other news services will be giving it the hillbilly twist, medieval superstition messing up the atomic world. What dumb jerks these dumb jerks are! You stay off that line. Find yourself a weepy individual slant on blood-sucking and sob me about three thousand words. And keep your expense account down—you just can't work a big swindle sheet out of that kind of agricultural slum.'

So I saddles my convertible, Shellinger thought morosely, and I tools off to the pappy-mammy country where nobody speaks to strangers nohow 'specially now, 'cause the vampire done got to three young 'uns already.' And nobody will tell me the names of those three kids or whether any of them are still alive; and Randall's wires keep asking when I'll start sending usable copy; and I still can't find one loquacious Louise in the whole country. Wouldn't even have known of this cross-country hunt if I hadn't begun to wonder where all the men in town had disappeared to on such an unappetising, rainy evening.

The road was bad in second, but it was impossible in almost any other gear. The ruts weren't doing the springs any good, either. Shellinger rubbed moisture off the glass with his handkerchief and wished he had another pair of headlights. He could hardly see.

That dark patch ahead, for instance. Might be one of the vampire posse. Might be some beast driven out of cover by the brush-beating. Might even be a little girl.

He ground into his brake. It was a girl. A little girl with dark hair and blue jeans. He twirled the crank and stuck his head out into the falling rain.

'Hey, kid. Want a lift?'

The child stooped slightly against the sombre background of night and decaying, damp countryside. Her eyes scanned the car, came back to his face and considered it. The kid had probably not known that this chromium-plated kind of postwar auto existed. She'd certainly never dreamed of riding in one. It would give her a chance to crow over the other kids in the 'tater patch.

Evidently deciding that he wasn't the kind of stranger her mother had warned her about and that it would be less uncomfortable in the car than walking in the rain and mud, she nodded. Very slowly, she came around the front and climbed in at his right.

'Thanks, mister,' she said.

Shellinger started again and took a quick, sidewise glance at the girl. Her blue jeans were raggedy and wet. She must be terribly cold and uncomfortable, but she wasn't going to let him know. She would bear up under it with the stoicism of the hill people.

But she was frightened. She sat hunched up, her hands folded neatly in her lap, at the far side of the seat right up against the door. What was the kid afraid of? Of course, the vampire!

'How far up do you go?' he asked her gently.

' 'Bout a mile and a half. But that way.' She pointed over her shoulder with a pudgy thumb. She was plump, much more flesh on her than most of these scrawny, share-cropped kids. She'd be beautiful, too, some day, if some illiterate lummox didn't cart her off to matrimony and hard work in a draughty cabin.

Regretfully, he manoeuvred around on the road, got the car turned and started back. He'd miss the hunters, but you couldn't drag an impressionable child into that sort of grim nonsense. He might as well take her home first. Besides, he wouldn't get anything out of those uncommunicative farmers with their sharpened stakes and silver bullets in their squirrel rifles.

'What kind of crops do your folks raise—tobacco or cotton?'

'They don't raise nothing yet. We just came here.'

'Oh.' That was right: she didn't have a mountain accent. Come to think of it, she was a little more dignified than most of the children he'd met in this neighbourhood. 'Isn't it a little late to go for a stroll? Aren't your folks afraid to let you out this late with a vampire around?'

She shivered. 'I—I'm careful,' she said at last.

Hey! Shellinger thought. Here was the human angle. Here was what Randall was bleating about. A frightened little girl with enough curiosity to swallow her big lump of fear and go out exploring on this night of all others. He didn't know how it fitted, just yet—but his journalistic nose was twitching. There was copy here; the basic, colourful human angle was sitting fearfully on his red leather seat.

'Do you know what a vampire is?'

She looked at him, startled, dropped her eyes and studied her folded hands for words. 'It's—it's like someone who needs people instead of meals.' A hesitant pause. 'Isn't it?'

'Ye-es.' That was good. Trust a child to give you a fresh viewpoint, unspoiled by textbook superstition. He'd use that —'People instead of meals.' 'A vampire is supposed to be a person who will be immortal—not die, that is—so long as he or she gets blood and life from living people. The only way you can kill a vampire—'

'You turn right here, mister.'

He pointed the car into the little branchlet of side-road. It was annoyingly narrow; surprised wet boughs tapped the windscreen, ran their leaves lazily across the car's fabric top. Once in a while, a tree top sneezed collected rain water down.

Shellinger pressed his face close to the windscreen and tried to decipher the picture of brown mud amid weeds that his headlights gave him. 'What a road! Your folks are really starting from scratch. Well, the only way to kill a vampire is with a silver bullet. Or you can drive a stake through the heart and bury it in a crossroads at midnight. That's what those men are going to do tonight if they catch it.' He turned his head as he heard her gasp. 'What's the matter—don't you like the idea?'

'I think it's horrid,' she told him emphatically.

'Why? How do you feel—live and let live?'

She thought it over, nodded, smiled. 'Yes. Live and let live. Live and let live. After all—' She was having difficulty finding the right words again. 'After all, some people can't help what they are. I mean,' very slowly, very thoughtfully, 'like if a person's a vampire, what can they do about it?'

'You've got a good point there, kid.' He went back to studying what there was of the road. 'The only trouble's this: if you believe in things like vampires, well, you don't believe in them good—you believe in them nasty. Those people back in the village who claim three children have been killed or whatever it was by the vampire, they hate it and want to destroy it. If there are such things as vampires—mind you, I said "if"—then, by nature, they do such horrible things that any way of getting rid of them is right. See?'

'No. You shouldn't drive stakes through people.'

Shellinger laughed. 'I'll say you shouldn't. Never could like that deal myself. However, if it were a matter of a vampire to me or mine, I think I could overcome my squeamishness long enough to do a little roustabout work on the stroke of twelve.'

He paused and considered that this child was a little too intelligent for her environment. She didn't seem to be bollixed with superstitions as yet, and he was feeding her *Shellinger on Black Magic*. That was vicious. He continued soberly, 'The difficulty with those beliefs is that a bunch of grown men who hold them are spread across the countryside tonight because they think a vampire is on the loose. And they're likely to flush some poor hobo and finish him off gruesomely for no other reason than that he can't give a satisfactory explanation for his presence in the fields on a night like this.'

Silence. She was considering his statement. Shellinger liked her dignified, thoughtful attitude. She was a bit more at ease, he noticed, and was sitting closer to him. Funny how a kid could sense that you wouldn't do her any harm. Even a country kid. Especially a country kid, come to think of it, because they lived closer to nature or something.

He had won her confidence, though, and consequently rewon his. A week of living among thin-lipped ignoramuses who had been not at all diffident in showing *their* disdain had made him a little uncertain. This was better. And he'd finally got a line on the basis of a story.

Only he'd have to dress it up. In the story, she'd be an ordinary hill-billy kid, much thinner, much more unapproachable; and the quotes would all be in 'mountain' dialect.

Yes, he had the human interest stuff now.

She had moved closer to him again, right against his side. Poor kid! His body warmth made the wet coldness of her jeans a little less uncomfortable. He wished he had a heater in the car.

The road disappeared entirely into tangled bushes and gnarly trees. He stopped the car.

'You don't live here? This place looks as if nothing human's been around for years.'

He was astonished at the uncultivated desolation.

'Sure I live here, mister,' her warm voice said at his ear. 'I live in that little house over there.'

'Where?' He rubbed at the windscreen and strained his vision over the sweep of headlights. 'I don't see any house. Where is it?'

'There.' A plump hand came up and waved at the night ahead. 'Over there.'

'I still can't see—' The corner of his right eye had casually noticed that the palm of her hand was covered with fine brown hair.

Strange, that.

Was covered with fine brown hair. Her palm!

'What *was* that you remembered about the shape of her teeth?' his mind shrieked. He started to whip his head around, to get another look at her teeth. But he couldn't.

Because her teeth were in his throat.

Gabriel-Ernest

SAKI

The werewolf also looms large as a popular figure in modern horror stories and films: although this creature of the night brought into being by the full moon has always proved particularly difficult to portray in a realistic way on the screen. The very idea of the werewolf is a bizarre one—that of a person being able to change into a wolf and back again—and this has resulted in a number of very extraordinary-looking beasts in the pictures I have seen. No such problem arises with the written word, though, for the reader can create absolute authenticity in his imagination without any need for make-up or trick photography. In the story here the author, Saki, has given us a particularly fascinating picture of the werewolf by restraining his description, yet hinting at enough to let the mind's eye get really busy. "Gabriel-Ernest", wherever he is, is not a boy I should care to encounter by moonlight!

'There is a wild beast in your woods,' said the artist Cunningham, as he was being driven to the station. It was the only remark he had made during the drive, but as Van Cheele had talked incessantly his companion's silence had not been noticeable.

'A stray fox or two and some resident weasels. Nothing more formidable,' said Van Cheele. The artist said nothing.

'What did you mean about a wild beast?' said Van Cheele later, when they were on the platform.

'Nothing. My imagination. Here is the train,' said Cunningham.

That afternoon Van Cheele went for one of his frequent rambles through his woodland property. He had a stuffed bittern in his study, and knew the names of quite a number of wild flowers, so his aunt had possibly some justification in describing him as a great naturalist. At any rate, he was a great walker. It was his custom to take mental notes of everything he saw during his walks, not so much for the purpose of assisting contemporary science as to provide topics for conversation afterwards. When the bluebells began to show themselves in flower he made a point of informing everyone of the fact; the season of the year might have warned his hearers of the likelihood of such an occurrence, but at least they felt that he was being absolutely frank with them.

What Van Cheele saw on this particular afternoon was, however, something far removed from his ordinary range of experience. On a shelf of smooth stone overhanging a deep pool in the hollow of an oak coppice a boy of about sixteen lay asprawl, drying his wet brown limbs luxuriously in the sun. His wet hair, parted by a recent dive, lay close to his head, and his light-brown eyes, so light that there was an almost tigerish gleam in them, were turned towards Van Cheele with a certain lazy watchfulness. It was an unexpected apparition, and Van Cheele found himself engaged in the novel process of thinking before he spoke. Where on earth could this wild-looking boy hail from? The miller's wife had lost a child some two months ago, supposed to have been swept away by the mill-race, but that had been a mere baby, not a half-grown lad.

'What are you doing there?' he demanded.

'Obviously, sunning myself,' replied the boy.

'Where do you live?'

'Here, in these woods.'

'You can't live in the woods,' said Van Cheele.

'They are very nice woods,' said the boy, with a touch of patronage in his voice.

'But where do you sleep at night?'

'I don't sleep at night; that's my busiest time.'

Van Cheele began to have an irritated feeling that he was grappling with a problem that was eluding him.

'What do you feed on?' he asked.

'Flesh,' said the boy, and he pronounced the word with slow relish, as though he were tasting it.

'Flesh! What flesh?'

'Since it interests you, rabbits, wild-fowl, hares, poultry, lambs in their season, children when I can get any; they're usually too well locked in at night, when I do most of my hunting. It's quite two months since I tasted child-flesh.'

Ignoring the chaffing nature of the last remark, Van Cheele tried to draw the boy on the subject of possible poaching operations.

'You're talking rather through your hat when you speak of feeding on hares.' (Considering the nature of the boy's toilet, the smile was hardly an apt one.) 'Our hillside hares aren't easily caught.'

'At night I hunt on four feet,' was the somewhat cryptic response.

'I suppose you mean that you hunt with a dog?' hazarded Van Cheele.

The boy rolled slowly over on to his back, and laughed a weird low laugh, that was pleasantly like a chuckle and disagreeably like a snarl.

'I don't fancy any dog would be very anxious for my company, especially at night.'

Van Cheele began to feel that there was something positively uncanny about the strange-eyed, strange-tongued youngster.

'I can't have you staying in these woods,' he declared authoritatively.

'I fancy you'd rather have me here than in your house,' said the boy.

The prospect of this wild, nude animal in Van Cheele's primly ordered house was certainly an alarming one.

'If you don't go I shall have to make you,' said Van Cheele.

The boy turned like a flash, plunged into the pool, and in a moment had flung his wet and glistening body halfway up the bank where Van Cheele was standing. In an otter the movement would not have been remarkable; in a boy Van Cheele found it sufficiently startling. His foot slipped as he made an involuntary backward movement, and he found himself almost prostrate on the slippery weed-grown bank, with those tigerish yellow eyes not very far from his own. Almost instinctively he half-raised his hand to his throat. The boy laughed again, a laugh in which the snarl had nearly driven out the chuckle, and then, with another of his astonishing lightning movements, plunged out of view into a yielding tangle of weed and fern.

'What an extraordinary wild animal!' said Van Cheele as he picked himself up. And then he recalled Cunningham's remark, 'There is a wild beast in your woods.'

Walking slowly homeward, Van Cheele began to turn over in his mind various local occurrences which might be traceable to the existence of this astonishing young savage.

Something had been thinning the game in the woods lately, poultry had been missing from the farms, hares were growing unaccountably scarcer, and complaints had reached him of lambs being carried off bodily from the hills. Was it possible that this wild boy was really hunting the countryside in company with some clever poacher dog? He had spoken of hunting 'four-footed' by night, but then, again, he had hinted strangely at no dog caring to come near him, 'especially at night'. It was certainly puzzling. And then, as Van Cheele ran his mind over the various depredations that had been committed during the last month or two, he came suddenly to a dead stop, alike in his walk and his speculations. The child missing from the mill two months ago—the accepted theory was that it had tumbled into the mill race and been swept away; but the mother had always declared she had heard a shriek on the hill side of the house, in the opposite direction from the water. It was unthinkable, of course, but he wished that the boy had not made that uncanny remark about child-flesh eaten two months ago. Such dreadful things should not be said even in fun.

Van Cheele, contrary to his usual wont, did not feel disposed to be communicative about his discovery in the wood. His position as a parish councillor and justice of the peace seemed somehow compromised by the fact that he was harbouring a personality of such doubtful repute on his property; there was even a possibility that a heavy bill of damages for raided lambs and poultry might be laid at his door. At dinner that night he was quite unusually silent.

'Where's your voice gone to?' said his aunt. 'One would think you had seen a wolf.'

Van Cheele, who was not familiar with the old saying, thought the remark rather foolish; if he *had* seen a wolf on his property his tongue would have been extraordinarily busy with the subject.

At breakfast next morning Van Cheele was conscious that his feeling of uneasiness regarding yesterday's episode had not wholly disappeared, and he resolved to go by train to the neighbouring cathedral town, hunt up Cunningham, and learn from him what he had really seen that had prompted the remark about a wild beast in the woods. With this resolution taken, his usual cheerfulness partially returned, and he hummed a bright little melody as he sauntered to the morning-room for his customary cigarette. As he entered the room the melody made way abruptly for a pious invocation. Gracefully asprawl on the ottoman, in an attitude of almost exaggerated repose, was the boy of the woods. He was drier than when Van Cheele had last seen him, but no other alteration was noticeable in his toilet.

'How dare you come here?' asked Van Cheele furiously.

'You told me I was not to stay in the woods,' said the boy calmly.

'But not to come here. Supposing my aunt should see you!'

And with a view to minimising that catastrophe Van Cheele hastily obscured as much of his unwelcome guest as possible under the folds of a *Morning Post*. At that moment his aunt entered the room.

'This is a poor boy who has lost his way—and lost his memory. He doesn't know who he is or where he comes from,' explained Van Cheele desperately, glancing apprehensively at the waif's face to see whether he was going to

add inconvenient candour to his other savage propensities.
Miss Van Cheele was enormously interested.

'Perhaps his underlinen is marked,' she suggested.

'He seems to have lost most of that, too,' said Van Cheele, making frantic little grabs at the *Morning Post* to keep it in its place.

A naked homeless child appealed to Miss Van Cheele as warmly as a stray kitten or derelict puppy would have done.

'We must do all we can for him,' she decided, and in a very short time a messenger, dispatched to the rectory, where a page-boy was kept, had returned with a suit of pantry clothes, and the necessary accessories of shirt, shoes, collar, etc. Clothed, clean, and groomed, the boy lost none of his uncanniness in Van Cheele's eyes, but his aunt found him sweet.

'We must call him something till we know who he really is,' she said. 'Gabriel-Ernest, I think; those are nice suitable names.'

Van Cheele agreed, but he privately doubted whether they were being grafted on to a nice suitable child. His misgivings were not diminished by the fact that his staid and elderly spaniel had bolted out of the house at the first incoming of the boy, and now obstinately remained shivering and yapping at the farther end of the orchard, while the canary, usually as vocally industrious as Van Cheele himself, had put itself on an allowance of frightened cheeps. More than ever he was resolved to consult Cunningham without loss of time.

As he drove off to the station his aunt was arranging that Gabriel-Ernest should help her to entertain the infant members of her Sunday-school class at tea that afternoon.

Cunningham was not at first disposed to be communicative.

'My mother died of some brain trouble,' he explained, 'so you will understand why I am averse to dwelling on anything of an impossibly fantastic nature that I may see or think that I have seen.'

'But what *did* you see?' persisted Van Cheele.

'What I thought I saw was something so extraordinary that no really sane man could dignify it with the credit of having actually happened. I was standing, the last evening I was with you, half-hidden in the hedgegrowth by the orchard gate, watching the dying glow of the sunset. Suddenly I became aware of a naked boy, a bather from some neighbouring pool, I took him to be, who was standing out on the bare hillside also watching the sunset. His pose was so suggestive of some wild faun of Pagan myth that I instantly wanted to engage him as a model, and in another moment I think I should have hailed him. But just then the sun dipped out of view, and all the orange and pink slid of the landscape, leaving it cold and grey. And at the same moment an astounding thing happened—the boy vanished too!'

'What! vanished away into nothing?' asked Van Cheele excitedly.

'No; that is the dreadful part of it,' answered the artist; 'on the open hillside where the boy had been standing a second ago, stood a large wolf, blackish in colour, with gleaming fangs and cruel, yellow eyes. You may think——'

But Van Cheele did not stop for anything as futile as thought. Already he was tearing at top speed towards the station. He dismissed the idea of a telegram. 'Gabriel-Ernest is a werewolf' was a hopelessly inadequate effort at conveying the situation, and his aunt would think it was a code message to which he had omitted to give her the key. His one hope was that he might reach home before sundown. The cab which he chartered at the other end of the railway journey bore him with what seemed exasperating slowness along the country roads, which were pink and mauve with the flush of the sinking sun. His aunt was putting away some unfinished jams and cake when he arrived.

'Where is Gabriel-Ernest?' he almost screamed.

'He is taking the little Toop child home,' said his aunt. 'It was getting so late, I thought it wasn't safe to let it go back alone. What a lovely sunset, isn't it?'

But Van Cheele, although not oblivious of the glow in the

western sky, did not stay to discuss its beauties. At a speed for which he was scarcely geared he raced along the narrow lane that led to the home of the Toops. On one side ran the swift current of the mill-stream, on the other rise the stretch of bare hillside. A dwindling rim of red sun showed still on the skyline, and the next turning must bring him in view of the ill-assorted couple he was pursuing. Then the colour went suddenly out of things, and a grey light settled itself with a quick shiver over the landscape. Van Cheele heard a shrill wail of fear, and stopped running.

Nothing was ever seen again of the Toop child or Gabriel-Ernest, but the latter's discarded garments were found lying in the road, so it was assumed that the child had fallen into the water, and that the boy had stripped and jumped in, in a vain endeavour to save it. Van Cheele and some workmen who were near by at the time testified to having heard a child scream loudly just near the spot where the clothes were found. Mrs Toop, who had eleven other children, was decently resigned to her bereavement, but Miss Van Cheele sincerely mourned her lost foundling. It was on her initiative that a memorial brass was put up in the parish church to 'Gabriel-Ernest, an unknown boy, who bravely sacrificed his life for another.'

Van Cheele gave way to his aunt in most things, but he flatly refused to subscribe to the Gabriel-Ernest memorial.

Sweets to the Sweet

ROBERT BLOCH

The witch is another figure that everyone has a mental picture of in their mind. The most popular idea is certainly that of the old crone with her pointed hat and flowing cloak riding across the sky on her broomstick. However, modern investigation has uncovered a lot of facts about witches, and while some of them may have been old and ugly, there were plenty who were young and attractive, too. For, if we are to accept this research, the real witches belonged to a secret organisation that worshipped the old gods of nature, and possessed the knowledge to work spells for both good and evil. The idea that they were all in league with the Devil really grew up during the superstitious past when our forebears were frightened of anything they thought was not quite normal or did not understand. As I live in a part of England that has a long tradition of witchcraft, I know that there is plenty of evidence of people today still practising the old witch ways and spells. And this is not just confined to the country: witch magic can work in towns and cities, too. In "Sweets to the Sweet", Robert Bloch, the famous American writer of creepy tales, tells a story of modern witchcraft at work—a story, I should add, that shows witch powers can be used by the young just as well as the old!

Irma didn't look like a witch.

She had small, regular features, a peaches-and-cream complexion, blue eyes and fair, almost ash-blonde hair. Besides, she was only eight years old.

'Why does he tease her so?' sobbed Miss Pall. 'That's where she got the idea in the first place—because he calls her a little witch.'

Sam Steever bulked his paunch back into the squeaky swivel chair and folded his hammy hands in his lap. His fat lawyer's mask was immobile, but he was really quite distressed.

Women like Miss Pall should never sob. Their glasses wiggle, their thin noses twitch, their creasy eyelids redden, and their stringy hair becomes disarrayed.

'Please, my dear, control yourself,' coaxed Sam Steever. 'Perhaps if we could just talk this whole thing over sensibly—'

'I don't care!' Miss Pall sniffled. 'I'm not going back there again. I can't stand it. There's nothing I can do. The man is your brother, and she's your brother's child. It's not my responsibility. I've tried—'

'Of course you've tried.' Sam Steever smiled benignly, as if Miss Pall were foreman of the jury. 'I quite understand. But I still don't see why you are so agitated, dear lady.'

Miss Pall removed her spectacles and dabbed at her eyes with a floral-print handkerchief. Then she deposited the soggy ball in her purse, snapped the catch, replaced her spectacles, and sat up straight.

'Very well, Mr Steever,' she said. 'I shall do my best to acquaint you with my reasons for quitting your brother's employ.'

She suppressed a tardy sniff.

'I came to John Steever two years ago in response to an advertisement for a housekeeper, as you know. When I found that I was to be governess to a motherless six-year-old child, I was at first distressed. I know nothing of the care of children.'

'John had a nurse the first six years,' Sam Steever nodded. 'You know Irma's mother died in childbirth.'

'I am aware of that,' said Miss Pall, primly. 'Naturally, one's heart goes out to a lonely, neglected little girl. And she was so terribly lonely, Mr Steever—if you could have seen her, moping around in the corners of that big, ugly old house—'

'I have seen her,' said Sam Steever hastily, hoping to forestall another outburst. 'And I know what you've done for Irma. My brother is inclined to be thoughtless, even a bit selfish at times. He doesn't understand.'

'He's cruel,' declared Miss Paul, suddenly vehement. 'Cruel and wicked. Even if he is your brother, I say he's no fit father for any child. When I came there, her little arms were black and blue from beatings. He used to take a belt—'

'I know. Sometimes I think John never recovered from the shock of Mrs Steever's death. That's why I was so pleased when you came, dear lady. I thought you might help the situation.'

'I tried,' Miss Pall whimpered. 'You know I tried. I never raised a hand to that child in two years, though many's the time your brother has told me to punish her. "Give the little witch a beating," he used to say. "That's all she needs—a good thrashing." And then she'd hide behind my back and whisper to me to protect her. But she wouldn't cry, Mr Steever. Do you know, I've never seen her cry.'

Sam Steever felt vaguely irritated and a bit bored. He wished the old hen would get on with it. So he smiled and oozed treacle. 'But just what is your problem, dear lady?'

'Everything was all right when I came there. We got along just splendidly. I started to teach Irma to read—and was surprised to find that she had already mastered reading. Your brother disclaimed having taught her, but she spent hours curled up on the sofa with a book. "Just like her," he used to say. "Unnatural little witch. Doesn't play with the other children. Little witch." That's the way he kept talking, Mr Steever. As if she were some sort of—I don't know what. And she so sweet and quiet and pretty!

'Is it any wonder she read? I used to be that way myself when I was a girl, because—but never mind.

'Still, it was a shock that day I found her looking through the *Encyclopedia Britannica*. "What are you reading, Irma?" I asked. She showed me. It was the article on Witchcraft.

'You see what morbid thoughts your brother had inculcated in her poor little head?

'I did my best. I went out and bought her some toys—she had absolutely nothing, you know; not even a doll. She didn't even know how to *play*! I tried to get her interested in some of the other little girls in the neighbourhood, but it was no use. They didn't understand her and she didn't understand them. There were scenes. Children can be cruel, thoughtless. And her father wouldn't let her go to public school. I was to teach her—

'Then I brought her the modelling clay. She liked that. She would spend hours just making faces with clay. For a child of six, Irma displayed real talent.

'We made little dolls together, and I sewed clothes for them. That first year was a happy one, Mr Steever. Particularly during those months when your brother was away in South America. But this year, when he came back—oh, I can't bear to talk about it!'

'Please,' said Sam Steever. 'You must understand. John is not a happy man. The loss of his wife, the decline of his import trade, and his drinking—but you know all that.'

'All I know is that he hates Irma,' snapped Miss Pall, suddenly. 'He hates her. He wants her to be bad, so he can whip her. "If you don't discipline the little witch, I shall," he always says. And then he takes her upstairs and thrashes her with his belt—you must do something, Mr Steever, or I'll go to the authorities myself.'

The crazy old biddy would do that, Sam Steever thought. Remedy—more treacle. 'But about Irma,' he persisted.

'She's changed, too. Ever since her father returned this year. She won't play with me any more, hardly looks at me. It is as though I failed her, Mr Steever, in not protecting her from that man. Besides—she thinks she's a witch.'

Crazy. Stark, staring crazy. Sam Steever creaked upright in his chair.

'Oh, you needn't look at me like that, Mr Steever. She'll tell you so herself—if you ever visited the house!'

He caught the reproach in her voice and assuaged it with a deprecating nod.

'She told me all right, if her father wants her to be a witch she'll be a witch. And she won't play with me, or anyone else, because witches don't play. Last Halloween she wanted me to give her a broomstick. Oh, it would be funny if it weren't so tragic. That child is losing her sanity.

'Just a week ago I thought she'd changed. That's when she asked me to take her to church one Sunday. "I want to see the baptism," she said. Imagine that—an eight-year-old interested in baptism! Reading too much, that's what does it.

'Well, we went to church and she was as sweet as can be, wearing her new blue dress and holding my hand. I was proud of her, Mr Steever, really proud.

'But after that, she went right back into her shell. Reading around the house, running through the yard at twilight and talking to herself.

'Perhaps it's because your brother wouldn't bring her a kitten. She was pestering him for a black cat, and he asked why, and she said, "Because witches always have black cats." Then he took her upstairs.

'I can't stop him, you know. He beat her again the night the power failed and we couldn't find the candles. He said she'd stolen them. Imagine that—accusing an eight-year-old child of stealing candles!

'That was the beginning of the end. Then today, when he found his hairbrush missing—'

'You say he beat her with his hairbrush?'

'Yes. She admitted having stolen it. Said she wanted it for her doll.'

'But didn't you say she has no dolls?'

'She made one. At least I think she did. I've never seen it—she won't show us anything any more; won't talk to us at table, just impossible to handle her.

'But this doll she made—it's a small one, I know, because at times she carries it tucked under her arm. She talks to it and pets it, but she won't show it to me or to him. He asked her about the hairbrush and she said she took it for the doll.

'Your brother flew into a terrible rage—he'd been drinking in his room again all morning; oh, don't think I don't know it!—and she just smiled and said he could have it now. She went over to her bureau and handed it to him. She hadn't harmed it in the least; some of the hair from his head was still in it, I noticed.

'But he snatched it up, and then he started to strike her about the shoulders with it, and he twisted her arm and then he—'

Miss Pall huddled in her chair and summoned great racking sobs from her thin chest.

Sam Steever patted her shoulder, fussing about her like an elephant over a wounded canary.

'That's all, Mr Steever. I came right to you. I'm not even going back to that house to get my things. I can't stand any more—the way he beat her—and the way she didn't cry, just giggled and giggled and giggled—sometimes I think she is a witch—that he made her into a witch—'

Sam Steever picked up the phone. The ringing had broken the relief of silence after Miss Pall's hasty departure.

'Hello—that you, Sam?'

He recognized his brother's voice, somewhat the worse for drink.

'Yes, John.'

'I suppose the old bat came running straight to you to shoot her mouth off.'

'If you mean Miss Pall, I've seen her, yes.'

'Pay no attention. I can explain everything.'

'Do you want me to stop in? I haven't paid you a visit in months.'

'Well—not right now. Got an appointment with the doctor this evening.'

'Something wrong?'

'Pain in my arm. Rheumatism or something. Getting a little diathermy. But I'll call you tomorrow.'

'Right.'

But John Steever did not call the next day. About supper time, Sam called him.

Surprisingly enough, Irma answered the phone. Her thin, squeaky little voice sounded faintly in Sam's ears.

'Daddy's upstairs sleeping. He's been sick.'

'Well, don't disturb him. What is it—his arm?'

'His back, now. He has to go to the doctor again in a little while.'

'Tell him I'll call tomorrow, then. Uh—everything all right, Irma? I mean, don't you miss Miss Pall?'

'No. I'm glad she went away. She's stupid.'

'Oh. Yes. I see. But you phone me if you want anything. And I hope your daddy's better.'

'Yes. So do I,' said Irma, and then she began to giggle, and then she hung up.

There was no giggling the following afternoon when John Steever called Sam at the office. His voice was sober—with the sharp sobriety of pain.

'Sam—for God's sake, get over here. Something's happening to me!'

'There's a client in the office, but I'll get rid of him. Say, wait a minute. Why don't you call the doctor?'

'That quack can't help me. He gave me diathermy for my arm and yesterday he did the same thing for my back.'

'Didn't it help?'

'The pain went away, yes. But it's back now. I feel—like I was being crushed. Squeezed, here in the chest. I can't breathe.'

'Sounds like pleurisy.'

'It isn't pleurisy. He examined me. Said I was sound as a dollar. No, there's nothing organically wrong. And I couldn't tell him the real cause.'

'Real cause?'

'Yes. The pins. The pins that little fiend is sticking into the doll she made. Into the arm, the back. And now heaven only knows how she's causing *this*.'

'John, you mustn't—'

'Oh, what's the use of talking? It's the doll all right, the one she made with the candle-wax and the hair from my brush. Oh—it hurts to talk—that cursed little witch! Hurry,

Sam. Promise me you'll do something—anything—get that doll from her—get that doll—'

Half an hour later, at four-thirty, Sam Steever entered his brother's house.

Irma opened the door.

It gave Sam a shock to see her standing there, smiling and unperturbed, pale blonde hair brushed immaculately back from the rosy oval of her face. She looked just like a little doll. A little doll—

'Hello, Uncle Sam.'

'Hello, Irma. Your daddy called me, did he tell you? He said he wasn't feeling well—'

'I know. But he's all right now. He's sleeping.'

Something happened to Sam Steever; a drop of ice-water trickled down his spine.

'Sleeping?' he croaked. 'Upstairs?'

Before she opened her mouth to answer he was bounding up the steps to the second floor, striding down the hall to John's bedroom.

John lay on the bed. He was asleep, and only asleep. Sam Steever noted the regular rise and fall of his chest as he breathed. His face was calm, relaxed.

Then the drop of ice-water evaporated, and Sam could afford to smile and murmur, 'Nonsense,' under his breath as he turned away.

As he went downstairs he hastily improvised plans. A six-month vacation for his brother; avoid calling it a 'cure'. An orphanage for Irma; give her a chance to get away from this morbid old house. . . .

He paused halfway down the stairs. Peering over the banister through the twilight he saw Irma on the sofa, cuddled up like a little white ball. She was talking to something she cradled in her arms, rocking it to and fro.

Then there was a doll, after all.

Sam Steever tiptoed very quietly down the stairs and walked over to Irma.

'Hello,' he said.

5

She jumped. Both arms rose to cover completely whatever it was she had been fondling. She squeezed it tightly.

Sam Steever thought of a doll being squeezed across the chest—

'Daddy's better now, isn't he?' lisped Irma.

'Yes, much better.'

'I knew he would be.'

'But I'm afraid he's going to have to go away for a rest. A long rest.'

A smile flittered through the mask. 'Good,' said Irma.

'Of course,' Sam went on, 'you couldn't stay here all alone. I was wondering—maybe we could send you off to school, or to some kind of a home—'

Irma giggled. 'Oh, you needn't worry about me,' she said. She shifted about on the sofa as Sam sat down, then sprang up quickly as he came close to her.

Her arms shifted with the movement, and Sam Steever saw a pair of tiny legs dangling down below her elbow. There were trousers on the legs, and little bits of leather for shoes.

'What's that you have, Irma?' he asked. 'Is it a doll?' He extended his hand.

She pulled it back.

'You can't see it,' she said.

'But I want to. Miss Pall said you made such lovely ones.'

'Miss Pall is stupid. So are you. Go away.'

'Please, Irma. Let me see it.'

But even as he spoke, Sam Steever was staring at the top of the doll, momentarily revealed, when she backed away. It was a head all right, with wisps of hair over a white face. Dusk dimmed the features, but Sam recognised the eyes, the nose, the chin—

He could keep up the pretence no longer.

'Give me that doll, Irma!' he snapped. 'I know what it is. I know *who* it is—'

For an instant the mask slipped from Irma's face, and Sam Steever stared into naked fear.

She knew. She knew he knew.

Then, just as quickly, the mask was replaced.

Irma was only a sweet, spoiled, stubborn little girl as she shook her head merrily and smiled with impish mischief in her eyes.

'Oh, Uncle Sam,' she giggled. 'You're so silly! Why, this isn't a *real* doll.'

Irma giggled once more, raising the figure as she spoke. 'Why, it's only—candy!' Irma said.

'Candy?'

Irma nodded. Then, very swiftly, she slipped the tiny head of the image into her mouth.

And bit it off.

There was a single piercing scream from upstairs.

As Sam Steever turned and ran up the steps, little Irma, still gravely munching, skipped out of the front door and into the night beyond.

The Witch of Ramoth

MARK VAN DOREN

In this second story with witchcraft as its theme, the central figure is cast as the traditional old crone, but seen to be busy with her spells in the heart of a modern housing community. It is a tale at first whimsical, but there is an icy undercurrent which slowly intrudes as the plot unfolds. The author, Mark Van Doren, is a distinguished American professor and prize-winning poet, and his eerie description of Tom and Abigail's encounter with "The Witch of Ramoth" makes for one of those stories that remains in the memory long after you have finished reading it.

It was cold at the corner of Springfield and Willow. A wind always blew there, but this time it was bitter, and fluttered the small blue fire under the tray of chestnuts an old woman was keeping warm for the children who passed.

But the children of Ramoth had never seen chestnuts being roasted before. It was not a city, it was not even a big town, and old women at street corners were an unusual sight.

'Chestnuts, chestnuts!' this one cried in a cracked voice that the wind blew away up Willow Street as if it were a puff of steam escaping from her instead of from the stove she tended.

And the children who were not afraid of her laughed—the girls because she was so ugly, the boys because they didn't know what it was she roasted. 'Buckeyes!' they shouted. 'Hot buckeyes! Odd or even—burn your hands to death with red-hot buckeyes!'

She paid no attention to this, but poked at the brown nuts to keep them from getting scorched, or peered from under the brim of her wide hat to see who was coming next down Springfield Street or Willow Street. She seemed to be expecting someone in particular, someone who would buy.

Someone, anyway, who would stop and look respectfully at what she sold.

When Tom and Abigail appeared, swinging the empty lunch boxes their mother had filled that morning, the old woman clapped her dark hands and pulled the torn cloak tighter about her neck. They looked very small in the dark, and indeed they were only children; but nobody else was visible at this moment, and she was as glad to see them as she would be if she had been expecting them. Perhaps she had.

But they were arguing, and didn't even see her there at the cold corner as they turned up Willow Street. The street climbed for a block, then levelled off for a while in the direction of the high mountains east of Ramoth. Their house was in the second block. Number 27.

They didn't see her because they were glaring at each other as they passed.

'You did too!' said Tom.

'I did not!' said Abigail, who was younger. 'I didn't, and you know it. When we get home—'

The old woman, looking after them as they stared up the walk, heard this, then heard no more. She reached over, raked the chestnuts into a row, picked out the fourth one, put it in her pocket, and turned her head the other way. The fourth chestnut had been burning hot, but her fingers were used to this, and so were the thick folds of her skirt. She smacked her lips, rubbed her nose thoughtfully, and settled down to wait for further people, young or old, to come along and notice her. Yet no one came.

'What's that burning?' said Abigail at the top of the rise. A whiff of chestnut smoke had followed them, blown all this way by the wind. 'Is there a fire?'

'Oh,' said Tom, who like his sister had already forgotten being angry, 'leaves. Or something. I don't see—'

He stopped suddenly.

'See what?' said Abigail, loosening the muffler at her throat.

'Do *you*?'

He was staring like a ghost.

'Who *is* it? What's the matter?'

'Look. Our house.'

It wasn't there. The fourth house from the corner, between Williamses and Rortys, wasn't there with its steep roof—the steepest roof in the row, they had always been proud to say, and there was no such roof. No such house. No lighted window on the near side as you came, with Tiger sitting on the sill pretending he hadn't missed anybody; with Father behind him, walking up and down impatient for supper; and with Mother in the kitchen, out of sight, getting it ready.

'Tom.'

He didn't hear.

'Tom! There isn't even a place for it. Nothing's happened to it. It didn't burn. It isn't—it simply—'

Abigail's teeth chattered so that she couldn't go on.

'No vacant lot,' said Tom as if to himself. 'You would think it never *had* been there. Rortys is where it was, and Williamses. They haven't changed. But they're next door to one another. The block—it hasn't changed either—hasn't shortened or anything—except—'

He couldn't say any more, nor could his sister.

They looked desperately at each other, doubting their very selves. Tom felt his feet tingle, and then his scalp; and he thought Abigail did too, for she stamped once or twice, gently, and rubbed the top of her head. But he wouldn't ask.

Mr Thorne—Mary's father, down the street—was coming now. Both of them saw him, tall beneath the next lamp, and decided they were glad. If anything had happened, he would know. He would see them; he would say—

But the serious Mr Thorne, more serious than ever, went by without a word. They had stepped off the walk to let him pass, and he had passed; but not like one who saw them there.

'Mr Thorne!'

Abigail was running after him. But Tom caught up with

her and held her, shaking his head. They would cross over, she understood him to mean, and find out for themselves.

Even then they knew Mr Thorne hadn't heard.

They crossed Willow Street, scuffling through the dead leaves, and stopped fearfully in front of Williamses' house. Number 25—there it was, so why were they afraid?

They hurried on, looking straight ahead. Number 29—nothing at Rortys was different either. And yet—

'Tom!' whispered Abigail. 'Why was it we didn't make any noise going through those leaves? We didn't. I'm sure.'

'Be still.'

The Rortys' porch light had come on, and Mrs Rorty was at the open door, glancing up and down the street.

'Mrs Rorty!' called Tom, not very loud. But loud enough for her to know he was there. If he was.

She stepped to the edge of the porch, but not to answer anybody. She leaned out, holding on to a post, and studied the darkness right and left. It was time for Mr Rorty to come home. More than time, perhaps, for she seemed anxious.

Before Tom could prevent it, Abigail dashed forward out of the dark and reached up to give a pull at Mrs Rorty's apron, a red one with a pattern of large flowers.

She grasped it firmly, or thought she did; and felt nothing. Nothing at all. The goods didn't gather where her thumb and fingers closed.

Abigail screamed, or thought she did, and ran back to where Tom, reaching for her mouth, covered it with both his hands.

'You mustn't,' he said. But she could tell. He too was terrified.

They watched Mrs Rorty go in. As she was about to close the door, however, she opened it again so that Ranger could come out. Old Ranger, rheumatic on the wooden steps—*he* would sniff at them at least, and wag his heavy tail, and wait patiently to be petted.

But not so. Even when they called him he had no curiosity;

and Abigail had to step aside for him as he lumbered towards the kerb.

The porch light went out, and they could no longer see each other's eyes. They could only hear Ranger among the leaves, starting and stopping, then starting on again, his huge paws making an absurd, solemn sound in the dry remnants of elm.

Abigail put her hand in Tom's.

'What'll we do?' She was crying.

'Walk up and down a while. What else? Maybe it will—maybe we are—'

'What?'

'Come on. We'll walk—well, anywhere. I don't feel tired. Do you?'

'No.'

'Or cold?'

'Not a bit.'

It was strange, thought Abigail, how warm she felt all over, and how light. How clear their voices sounded to each other, how low and clear, how separate and natural; yet no one else could hear them. How easily they moved together, their hands swinging at their sides, as the moon rose and showed them Ramoth Mountain.

'Shall we go there?' she said.

In no time they were among the giant pines. The white moon, feeling its way down through the shaggy tops, found a fox off to their left—a startled fox, with one foot lifted, that seemed unable to run. But not because of them. It was the sudden light that kept him there, his foot curled at his breast, while they fumbled closer to each other and went on.

Owls whimpered, but not at them, and when they heard something heavy bounding through the underbrush they knew they hadn't startled it.

'I'll tell you,' said Tom. 'Echo Ledge. Listen—it's over there—if *it* doesn't answer—'

He put his hands to his mouth and shouted 'Hey!'

No sound came back.

'Twenty-seven!'

Only a twig snapped somewhere

Abigail knew he was shaking all over. He had counted on the echo; he had been sure of that.

'Let's go home,' he said turning and running.

'Wait!' The woods were so thick, so dark now in spite of the moon.

He waited till she found him, then caught her hand. 'Come on. I didn't mean go *home*, but—'

'Oh, let's do!' Maybe it would be there this time.

But it wasn't, and she thought Tom didn't even turn his head to see. The Williamses' shades were up, and Lottie was practising at the piano. They could see her through the panes. Between here and the Rortys—what? A little space, just big enough for a car. All their house folded away—all of it, with Mother and Father and Tiger, and two small rooms upstairs. Their own rooms. Pitch dark, of course, because— but how could they be either dark or light?

Abigail burst into tears, it was so hard to talk even to herself. She said impossible things.

'Don't cry,' said Tom. 'We'll go on down to Springfield Street—at least that far—then maybe—'

'What?'

He still had hold of her hand when they reached the corner and saw an old woman bent over a smoking tray of brown nuts.

'Who's that?'

Abigail must have been nervous, or afraid. Otherwise she wouldn't have spoken so loud. For the old woman looked up.

'And who are you?' The sickle of her nose, curving down as she grinned, almost cleft her lips in two.

It was Tom who realised it first. 'You *heard* my sister? You see *us?*'

'Why not, why not! Are you so hard to look at then? Those'—for Tom was staring into the tray—'are chestnuts. Will you buy?'

But the boy and girl were thinking about the whiff of

smoke—this smoke—that they had smelled at the top of the hill. It was when they first had *noticed*. It wouldn't be there now. It hadn't been when they came down.

They were turning, they were running up again.

'Will you buy?'

It was so much like a command that Tom at least looked back. She was poking the chestnuts. She was putting them in a row.

'Wait,' he called to Abigail, who was not yet out of sight. 'We ought to.'

'Don't you *want* to?' That hideous face—why couldn't he look away?

'Yes,' he said, 'I do. But how much? I haven't any money. I could go and get some.'

'Where?'

He pointed over Abigail's head. 'Up there. That is, if—'

'Then I'll wait.'

She made a gap in the row, wide enough for one more chestnut, and thrust an arm down among the wrinkles of her skirt. 'But hurry. I haven't much more time.'

'I will, if I can find—'

'You can. You will. Supper's ready, and they're worried. The great cat, too. You're fifteen seconds late. But hurry back. All of these—you can have them for a dime. The little girl—will she wait here with me? She won't? A wild thing!'

For Abigail had long been out of hearing. She knew, and Tom knew, what would be up there.

Twilight Play

AUGUST DERLETH

The early evening is invariably a strange time which can have the most surprising effects on the mind. What with the night falling and the shadows lengthening, there is something a bit adventurous about being out alone, even a little dangerous, too. That applies to any age group, of course, because the mind can be at its most imaginative then, making something out of nothing. Or perhaps something out of something? August Derleth, the author of this next story, was one of the people who introduced me to the many facets of the ghost and horror story, and he always had a predilection for night-time tales, particularly because he had very vivid memories of his own childhood in the strange, dark winters which are peculiar to the countryside of Wisconsin in America where he was born. He had a wealth of stories about the games he and his friends used to get up to in the neighbouring fields and forest-land, and drew on these to write what I believe is one of his best short stories, "Twilight Play". There is certainly something of Mr Derleth in young Donald, but whether he really had a secret friend like Hawk I would not like to say.

In the evening it was playtime for one precious hour before bedtime, and, as usual, Donald ran into the park to the place of the mounds, where darkness already scouted the last sunlight.

'Hawk!' he called softly. 'Hawk!'

No one answered him. In the midst of an oak an owl keened softly, its thin wailing sad and lonely. Over in the fields larks and robins carolled; on the edge of the park three mourning doves sobbed.

He sat down on the thunderbird mound and waited.

The evening drew in. The long shadows of the park grew darker, almost concealing him. Larksong and robins' carolling diminished, and a nighthawk rose up to circle and spurt high into the evening's blue, sky-coasting down with a harsh *zoom* of air in its wings. The streetlights came on at the corners, but no light strayed to the mounds.

'Hawk!' he called impatiently. 'I know you're hiding. Come on.'

And Hawk was there, as always, coming like a shadow out of the darkness. His luminous eyes shone in the evening, startling Donald.

'You can do it every time,' said Donald in admiration.

In a moment they were at play—riding imaginary horses around the mounds, doing Hawk's special dances together: the war dance and the moon dance and the nightbird and the thunderbird dances, playing with intense solemnity, broken only occasionally by an excited cry from Donald. The night crept in, following orange and magenta afterglow down the west, and any moment now it would be time for Donald and Hawk to go in. But the play went on, though the very air seemed to be waiting for the sound of Donald's mother's voice calling him.

From the fence north of the mounds, separating the park from the long wooded lawns and the distant house rose the detested voice of Archer Connelly.

'Yah, Sissy Carstair! What d'you think you're doing?'

'None of your business,' said Donald, faltering.

Archer fingered a sharply pointed stone. 'Don't you talk to me like that, you guttersnipe!'

'Just let me alone and mind your own business,' said Donald.

He was properly aggrieved. Four out of six nights Archer Connelly came to lord it over them—Archer, who had everything his parents' money could buy, who was too good to play with poor children, but who could never let them alone. Meeting them on the street, he ran them off; at school he tormented them, and, since his father sat on the board of education, teachers tried not to see Archer's misdeeds. Even here, in the park, he could not keep from plaguing them by every means within his power.

'Your pants got holes in, Sissy Carstair,' he said.

'They're all right to play in,' said Donald.

' 'Cause you haven't any others, that's why,' jeered Archer.

A screen-door slammed and someone called, 'Archer!'

Archer flashed a glance around towards the house. Then he turned and flung the stone in his fingers; it caught Donald in the small of his back. He cried out and stumbled. Straightening up, he faced Archer's laughter. Instinctively, he reached for a stick to throw, but then he saw Archer's mother coming down towards the fence.

'Archer, come away from there,' she was saying. 'Haven't I told you not to associate with those children?'

Donald dropped his stick, cowed.

'I wasn't playing with him. I was just watching. He plays like a rummy,' said Archer, walking away with her.

Donald looked around, but Hawk was gone. He knew he would be. Almost every time Archer came, Hawk went. Donald reflected ruefully that Hawk wouldn't stay to listen to Archer, or to wait for the stone or the stick or whatever Archer might throw. Hawk went. Hawk had pride. He could just see Hawk's dark face with his tight lips and his black eyes lifting and turning away. Donald was ashamed of himself. But he was stubborn, too. Why should he run from Archer Connelly? Why should he?

'Don-ald!'

'Coming.'

He got up and sought vainly in the shadows. 'Good-night, Hawk. See you tomorrow,' he said. The screech owl in the oak wailed, and he ran home, across the bear mound, across the man mound, along the thunderbird mound, past the oak grove, along the rows of maples and elms, past the bandstand and the ice-cream stand, and across the road to the little house on the corner which was home.

'And did you have a good time?' his mother asked.

'Yes, 'cept for that old Archer.'

'Oh, don't pay any attention to him.'

'I don't, 'cept he throws stones an' tonight he hit me—an' he scares Hawk away,' he added as an afterthought.

'Who's Hawk?'

'You know, I told you.'

'Oh, the boy whose daddy bought him that nice Indian outfit.'

'Uh-huh.' He began to talk animatedly. 'He's got a tomahawk even, an' he just calls himself Red Hawk, that's his name, an' he can tell stories an' do dances . . .'

'What kind of stories?'

'Oh, like fairy tales. How he can change into a big hawk an' go hunting . . .'

'Is he older than you are?'

'He's bigger. He's a lot bigger. But you know what—he can come into the park an' he never makes a sound. Just like a real Indian. He can come right up behind me an' I never know he's there an' sometimes he scares me, he comes so quick. An' his mother never calls him!'

'Where does he live?'

'I don't know. I never was at his house.'

'Well, run along to bed now. Just as long as he's nice, I guess it's all right to play with him. Maybe some day your daddy'll get you an Indian suit, too.'

'Oh, will he, Ma, will he?'

'If you're good, maybe. We'll see. Maybe at Christmas . . .'

'I'll be good, Ma. I'm good.'

'And he is good, too,' said Mrs Carstair to her husband long after Donald had gone to bed, followed by his two sisters. 'I wish we could get him an Indian suit.'

'I don't know how. We've got all we can do to make ends meet. Anyway, I don't know what kid in town's got an outfit like that one. And the town isn't that big that I couldn't find one. With a name like that, too—Red Hawk.'

'It's the name of an old Sauk chieftain's son. You know, they used to have their village around here somewhere. Didn't they dig up his bones somewhere in town?'

'Oh, yes, that's town history. You can hear that every so often.'

'It's just the sort of thing some kid would pick up and use. It helps to point up everything we can't do for him, that's all.' She shrugged. 'I wish somebody could do something with that Connelly boy.'

'There's no use starting on that again. His parents aid and abet him, and you can't get to them.'

Next evening Hawk came a little earlier. It was an evening with a sickle of new moon low in the west, very beautiful to see among the dark trees silhouetted against the evening heaven. Donald confided eagerly that his parents might get him an Indian suit, too, not as nice or as complete as Hawk's, but just the same, a suit; they could play together at Hawk's games then with so much more gusto.

Archer came earlier, too.

'Who's that you're playing with?' he demanded suspiciously, leaning on the fence.

'He's my friend.'

'"He's my friend",' mimicked Archer. 'What's his name?'

'That's for me to know and you to find out.'

'You better tell me, Sissy Carstair, or you know what you'll get.'

'Try and make me,' said Donald defiantly.

'Hawk,' said Hawk like a short bark.

'That's not a name,' said Archer.

'It is so a name, Archer Connelly,' said Donald.

'Is not.'

'Is too.'

'I know better. You tell that Hawk friend of yours that all the new boys in this town have to come see me.'

Hawk made a sound deep in his throat like an angry dog.

'You better look out, Archer Connelly, or Hawk'll get mad. And when he gets mad, he gets awful mad. You'll be sorry.'

' "You'll be sorry", ' mimicked Archer again. 'Is he another one of those poor people like you?'

'What's wrong with poor people?' demanded Donald.

'You ought to know. Do you hear me, Hawk? Are you poor, too?'

Hawk made a growling sound.

'I guess if you weren't poor you wouldn't be playing with Sissy Carstair.' He looked back at Donald. 'What were you playing?'

'Rain dance.'

'What kind of a game is that?'

'It's a game; it's Hawk's game,' said Donald.

'Did you ever look funny jumping around like that! You're just crazy, Donald Carstair. And that Hawk boy, too.'

'You don't have to watch us.'

'I can watch all I please. This is our fence. If you don't like it, you can go somewhere else, and see if I care.'

The inevitable Mrs Connelly appeared out of the darkness and seized Archer, pausing only long enough to berate Donald and Hawk for 'keeping Archer out'.

Donald looked at Hawk. This time, for once, Hawk had not run away. Hawk's eyes looked soberly back at him; they were strange eyes, burning as if there were fire in them. Hawk said nothing, but sat quite tense, looking at him, as if trying to find out what he was thinking without asking.

'I can't help it if I'm poor,' volunteered Donald. 'Can you?'

Hawk shook his head sympathetically. But he had a suggestion to make. He knew a game the old witch-man of the tribe had taught him, he said. It was a game of getting even with boys like Archer. You pretended you had him helpless, at your mercy; there he was, all tied up, staked to the ground and tied to the stakes; then you imagined you were a hawk, and he was a mouse or something, and you came down out of the sky and you tore him to pieces. They could pretend Archer was the mouse.

In a moment Donald forgot his hurt and was engrossed in the wonderful pastime of pretending Archer Connelly was staked out on the thunderbird mound and being torn to pieces by Hawk and himself, also a hawk, and Archer was begging him to save his life, promising he would never do it again, but it made no difference, they tore him to pieces just the same, which served that old Archer right. At this they played diligently until Mrs Carstair called Donald home from the night-held park.

'Good-night, Hawk,' called Donald over his shoulder. He could just see Hawk standing there on the thunderbird mound—one moment he was there, and the next he was gone. Donald was filled to bursting with admiration for the way Hawk could move without a sound.

On the third evening, Archer Connelly, moved in the depths of his narrow, selfish soul by envy of Donald's manifest happiness, determined to avenge himself on both the boys. He would give them enough of Indian games. He had invaded his father's collection of Indian arrowheads, and abstracted the most pointed. He discarded a bow and arrows for his sling-shot, which had hitherto done nothing more dangerous than bring low the songbirds which strayed over from the park. He went out early and lay concealed behind a syringa along the fence-line; from there he could see the mounds clearly enough.

He saw Donald coming, but Donald did not see him.

He waited, bitterly.

'Hawk,' called Donald softly. 'Hawk!'

There was no answer. No wonder, thought Archer; I could hardly even hear that. But he was patient, and waited with his intended victim. He meant to see from which direction the boy Hawk came, but the evening darkened the mounds quickly, even while the sun still shone redly on the distant hills to the west, and suddenly he saw that Hawk had come, dressed up once more in that silly Indian outfit with the feathers and skin of a bird on his back.

He shifted position slightly, carefully stretched his slingshot, and took aim with the sharpest of the arrowheads.

The first arrowhead caught Donald a glancing blow on his shoulder.

He half-turned, looking for Archer.

The second arrowhead struck him above one eye, gashing his skin so that blood began to run towards one eye.

'Archer!' he cried out. 'You hurt me.'

The third arrowhead cut into his side; Donald fell, crying.

'Sissy Carstair can't stand an Indian raid,' Archer shouted. He fitted another arrowhead to his sling and took aim at Hawk. 'And neither can Sissy Hawk,' he called. The arrowhead sped through the darkness, true over the mound, straight at Hawk, who stood unmoving to receive it.

The arrowhead struck him in the middle and went straight through him.

Donald cried out. 'Hawk! Hawk! You're hurt!'

But something terrible was happening to Hawk.

It was no longer Hawk who stood there. It was a great bird. Donald thought it was as if that bird-skin Hawk wore had just grown and covered him. In another instant the bird was up and away, flying towards Archer.

And then it came down at Archer, and Archer was screaming horribly.

Donald closed his eyes and ran blindly towards home.

It was almost midnight when Frank Carstair came home. His wife was still up.

'They got Mrs Connelly to bed at last. Gave her a sedative strong enough to knock out a horse. Ugh!' He shuddered.

'I had to give Donald something, too. Frank, what was it?'

'Donald stuck to his story?'

'Yes. It was a big bird, bigger than a man, he said. They questioned him until I had to stop them. He said the same thing every time. Did you see Archer?'

'As much as I could stand to look. God, honey—it was

awful! Just torn to pieces—both arms torn off, head, too.' He shook himself and grimaced.

'Where could Donald have got such an idea?' she asked.

'All those stories that other boy told him, I suppose.'

'Yes, of course. We'll have to keep him home a little more.' He looked speculatively towards the park. 'Donald's had enough Indian stories to last him for years. How's Connelly taking the shock?'

'He's hard.'

'But such a terrible thing. I don't understand how it could have happened. Was that a shot?'

'Yes. Some of them are out hunting.'

'Hunting? At this hour?'

'Yes. Birds. Big birds.'

'Let's get to bed, Frank. I'm exhausted. Put out the light, will you? Birds. What in the world for?'

'Because the coroner said Archer had been killed by a bird. The marks on his body were like a predatory bird's —only much larger. Claw marks, definitely. He said they were just exactly the kind of marks, only larger, of course —you don't suppose he met up with Donald's friend, do you?—the marks of a hawk.'

The light went out.

Mr Lupescu

ANTHONY BOUCHER

This story, too, is about a small boy's 'secret friend' and the world of seemingly carefree adventures which they enjoy together. But there is something sinister about young Bobby's friend, "Mr Lupescu", although maybe it has more to do with another unseen companion named Gorgo? In this short, beautifully constructed tale, Anthony Boucher shows himself a master of the macabre tale and builds up the tension to a really shattering climax.

The teacups rattled and flames flickered over the logs.
'Alan, I *do* wish you could do something about Bobby.'
'Isn't that rather Robert's place?'
'Oh, you know *Robert*. He's so busy doing good in nice abstract ways with committees in them.'
'And headlines.'
'He can't be bothered with things like Mr Lupescu. After all, Bobby's only his *son*.'
'And yours, Marjorie.'
'And mine. But things like this take a *man*, Alan.'
The room was warm and peaceful; Alan stretched his long legs by the fire and felt domestic. Marjorie was soothing even when she fretted. The firelight did things to her hair and the curve of her blouse.
A small whirlwind entered at high velocity and stopped only when Marjorie said, 'Bob-*by!* Say hello nicely to Uncle Alan.'
Bobby said hello and stood tentatively on one foot.
'Alan . . .' Marjorie prompted.
Alan sat up straight and tried to look paternal. 'Well, Bobby,' he said. 'And where are you off to in such a hurry?'
'See Mr Lupescu, 'f course. He usually comes afternoons.'

'Your mother's been telling me about Mr Lupescu. He must be quite a person.'

'Oh, gee, I'll say he is, Uncle Alan. He's got a great big red nose and red gloves and red eyes—not like when you've been crying but really red like yours 're brown—and little red wings that twitch, only he can't fly with them cause they're ruddermentary he says. And he talks like—oh, gee, I can't do it, but he's swell, he is.'

'Lupescu's a funny name for a fairy godfather, isn't it, Bobby?'

'Why? Mr Lupescu always says why do all the fairies have to be Irish because it takes all kinds, doesn't it?'

'Alan!' Marjorie said. 'I don't see that you're doing a *bit* of good. You talk to him seriously like that and you simply make him think it *is* serious. And you *do* know better, don't you, Bobby? You're just joking with us.'

'Joking? About *Mr Lupescu*?'

'Marjorie, you don't—listen, Bobby. Your mother didn't mean to insult you or Mr Lupescu. She just doesn't believe in what she's never seen, and you can't blame her. Now supposing you took her and me out in the garden and we could all see Mr Lupescu. Wouldn't that be fun?'

'Uh, uh.' Bobby shook his head gravely. 'Not for Mr Lupescu. He doesn't like people. Only little boys. And he says if I ever bring people to see him then he'll let Gorgo get me. G'bye now.' And the whirlwind departed.

Marjorie sighed. 'At least thank heavens for Gorgo. I never can get a very clear picture out of Bobby, but he says Mr Lupescu tells the most *terrible* things about him. And if there's any trouble about vegetables or brushing teeth all I have to say is *Gorgo* and hey presto!'

Alan rose. 'I don't think you need worry, Marjorie. Mr Lupescu seems to do more good than harm, and an active imagination is no curse to a child.'

'You haven't *lived* with Mr Lupescu.'

'To live in a house like this, I'd chance it,' Alan laughed. 'But please forgive me now—back to the cottage and the typewriter. Seriously, why don't you ask Robert to talk with him?'

Marjorie spread her hands helplessly.

'I know. I'm always the one to assume responsibilities. And yet you married Robert.'

Marjorie laughed. 'I don't know. Somehow there's something *about* Robert. . . .' Her vague gesture happened to include the original Degas over the fireplace, the sterling tea service, and even the liveried footman who came in at that moment to clear away.

Mr Lupescu was pretty wonderful that afternoon all right. He had a little kind of an itch like in his wings and they kept twitching all the time. Stardust, he said. It tickles. Got it up in the Milky Way. Friend of his has a wagon route up there.

Mr Lupescu had lots of friends and they all did something you wouldn't ever think of not in a squillion years. That's why he didn't like people because people don't do things you can tell stories about. They just work or keep house or are mothers or something.

But one of Mr Lupescu's friends now was captain of a ship only it went in time and Mr Lupescu took trips with him and came back and told you all about what was happening this very minute five hundred years ago. And another of the friends was a radio engineer only he could tune in on all the kingdoms of faery and Mr Lupescu would squidgle up his red nose and twist it like a dial and make noises like all the kingdoms of faery coming in on the set. And then there was Gorgo only he wasn't a friend, not exactly, not even to Mr Lupescu.

They'd been playing for a couple of weeks only it must've been really hours 'cause Mamselle hadn't yelled about supper yet but Mr Lupescu says Time is funny, when Mr Lupescu screwed up his red eyes and said, 'Bobby, let's go in the house.'

'But there's people in the house and you don't—'

'I know I don't like people. That's why we're going in the house. Come on, Bobby, or I'll—'

So what could you do when you didn't even want to hear him say Gorgo's name?

He went into Father's study through the French window and it was a strict rule that nobody went into Father's study, but rules weren't for Mr Lupescu.

Father was on the telephone telling somebody he'd try to be at luncheon but there was a committee meeting that same morning but he'd see. While he was talking Mr Lupescu went over to a table and opened a drawer and took something out.

When Father hung up he saw Bobby first and started to be very mad. He said, 'Young man, you've been trouble enough to your mother and me with all your stories about your red-winged Mr Lupescu, and now if you're to start bursting in—'

You have to be polite and introduce people. 'Father, this is Mr Lupescu. And see he does, too, have red wings.'

Mr Lupescu held out the gun he'd taken from the drawer and shot Father once right through the forehead. It made a little clean hole in front and a big messy hole at the back. Father fell down and was dead.

'Now, Bobby,' Mr Lupescu said, 'a lot of people are going to come here and ask you a lot of questions. And if you don't tell the truth about exactly what happened, I'll send Gorgo to fetch you.'

Then Mr Lupescu was gone through the French window on to the gravel path.

'It's a curious case, Lieutenant,' the medical examiner said. 'It's fortunate I've dabbled a bit in psychiatry; I can at least give you a lead until you get the experts in. The child's statement that his fairy godfather shot his father is obviously a simple flight-mechanism, susceptible of two interpretations. A, the father shot himself; the child was so horrified by the sight that he refused to accept it and invented this explanation. B, the child shot the father, let us say by accident, and shifted the blame to his imaginary scapegoat. B has of course its more sinister implications; if the child had resented his father and created an ideal substitute, he might make the substitute destroy the reality. . . . But there's the solution to your eye-witness testimony; which alternative is true, Lieutenant, I leave it up to your researches into motive and the evidence of ballistics and fingerprints. The angle of the wound jibes with either.'

The man with the red nose and eyes and gloves and wings walked down the back lane to the cottage. As soon as he got inside he took off his coat and removed the wings and the mechanism of strings and rubbers that had made them twitch. He laid them on top of the ready pile of kindling and lit the fire. When it was well started, he added the gloves. Then he took off the nose, kneaded the putty until the red of its outside vanished into the neutral brown of the mass, jammed it into a crack in the wall, and smoothed it over. Then he took the red-irised contact lenses out of his brown eyes and went into the kitchen, found a hammer, pounded them to powder, and washed the powder down the sink.

Alan started to pour himself a drink and found, to his pleased surprise, that he didn't especially need one. But he did feel tired. He could lie down and recapitulate it all, from the invention of Mr Lupescu (and Gorgo and the man with the Milky Way route) to today's success and on into the future when Marjorie, pliant, trusting Marjorie would be more desirable than ever as Robert's widow and heir. And Bobby would need a *man* to look after him.

Alan went into the bedroom. Several years passed by in the few seconds it took him to recognise what was waiting on the bed, but then Time is funny.

Alan said nothing.

'Mr Lupescu, I presume?' said Gorgo.

Silent Snow, Secret Snow

CONRAD AIKEN

From 'secret friends' it is no distance to the 'secret worlds' of the imagination where one can be anything one pleases. Perhaps the world may be far removed in the realms of fantasy, or much closer to reality as in this next tale by Conrad Aiken, built around the seemingly commonplace ingredient of snow—yet nonetheless magical in its possibilities. It is a particular pleasure for me to be able to include Mr Aiken's story in this book, for he is the father of Joan Aiken, who contributed an earlier story, and their inclusion together underlines what I have said about the delight in terror tales being passed from one generation to the next. Joan Aiken has herself told me how she grew up in a family where such stories were being written all the time, and it gave her the inspiration to put pen to paper when she was barely in her teens. My own son, Richard, is similarly showing a strong interest in the macabre, and I suspect many of my readers are only continuing the lead of those close to them. Long may it continue so!

I

Just why it should have happened, or why it should have happened just when it did, he could not, of course, possibly have said; nor perhaps could it even have occurred to him to ask. The thing was above all a secret, something to be preciously concealed from Mother and Father; and to that very fact it owed an enormous part of its deliciousness. It was like a peculiarly beautiful trinket to be carried unmentioned in one's trouser-pocket—a rare stamp, an old coin, a few tiny gold links found trodden out of shape on the path in the park, a pebble of carnelian, a sea shell distinguishable from all others by an unusual spot or stripe—and, as if it were any one of these, he carried around with him everywhere a warm and persistent and increasingly beautiful sense of possession. Nor was it only a sense of possession—it was also a sense of protection. It was as if, in some delightful way, his secret gave him a fortress, a wall behind which he could retreat into heavenly seclusion. This was almost the first thing he had noticed about it—apart from the oddness of the thing itself—and it was this that now again, for the fiftieth time, occurred to him, as he sat in the little schoolroom. It was the half hour for geography. Miss Buell was revolving with one finger, slowly, a huge terrestrial globe which had been placed on her desk. The green and yellow continents passed and repassed, questions were asked and answered, and now the little girl in front of him, Deirdre, who had a funny little constellation of freckles on the back of her neck, exactly like the Big Dipper, was standing up and telling Miss Buell that the equator was the line that ran round the middle.

Miss Buell's face, which was old and greyish and kindly, with grey stiff curls beside the cheeks, and eyes that swam very brightly, like little minnows, behind thick glasses, wrinkled itself into a complication of amusements.

'Ah! I see. The earth is wearing a belt, or a sash. Or someone drew a line round it!'

'Oh, no—not that—I mean—'

In the general laughter, he did not share, or only a very little. He was thinking about the Arctic and Antarctic regions, which of course, on the globe, were white. Miss Buell was now telling them about the tropics, the jungles, the steamy heat of equatorial swamps, where the birds and butterflies, and even snakes, were like living jewels. As he listened to these things, he was already, with a pleasant sense of half-effort, putting his secret between himself and the words. Was it really an effort at all? For effort implied something voluntary, and perhaps even something one did not especially want; whereas this was distinctly pleasant, and came almost of its own accord. All he needed to do was to think of that morning, the first one, and then of all the others—

But it was all so absurdly simple! It had amounted to so

little. It was nothing, just an idea—and just why it should have become so wonderful, so permanent, was a mystery—a very pleasant one, to be sure, but also, in an amusing way, foolish. However, without ceasing to listen to Miss Buell, who had now moved up to the north temperate zone, he deliberately invited his memory of the first morning. It was only a moment or two after he had woken up—or perhaps the moment itself. But was there, to be exact, an exact moment? Was one awake all at once? Or was it gradual? Anyway, it was after he had stretched a lazy hand up towards the head-rail, and yawned, and then relaxed again among his warm covers, all the more grateful on a December morning, that the thing had happened. Suddenly, for no reason, he had thought of the postman, he remembered the postman. Perhaps there was nothing so odd in that. After all, he heard the postman almost every morning in his life —his heavy boots could be heard clumping round the corner at the top of the little cobbled hill-street, and then, progressively nearer, progressively louder, the double knock at each door, the crossings and re-crossings of the street, till finally the clumsy steps came stumbling across to the very door, and the tremendous knock came which shook the house itself.

(Miss Buell was saying 'Vast wheat-growing areas in North America and Siberia.'

Deirdre had for the moment placed her left hand across the back of her neck.)

But on this particular morning, the first morning, as he lay there with his eyes closed, he had for some reason *waited* for the postman. He wanted to hear him come round the corner. And that was precisely the joke—he never did. He never came. He never had come—*round the corner*—again. For when at last the steps *were* heard, they had already, he was quite sure, come a little down the hill, to the first house; and even so, the steps were curiously different—they were softer, they had a new secrecy about them, they were muffled and indistinct; and while the rhythm of them was the same, it now said a new thing—it said peace, it said remoteness, it said cold, it said sleep. And he had understood the situation at once—nothing could have seemed simpler—there had been snow in the night, such as all winter he had been longing for; and it was this which had rendered the postman's first footsteps inaudible, and the later ones faint. Of course! How lovely! And even now it must be snowing—it was going to be a snowy day—the long white ragged lines were drifting and sifting across the street, across the faces of the old houses, whispering and hushing, making little triangles of white in the corners between cobblestones, seething a little when the wind blew them over the ground to a drifted corner; and so it would be all day, getting deeper and deeper and silenter and silenter.

(Miss Buell was saying 'Land of perpetual snow.')

All this time, of course (while he lay in bed), he had kept his eyes closed, listening to the nearer progress of the postman, the muffled footsteps thumping and slipping on the snow-sheathed cobbles; and all the other sounds—the double knocks, a frosty far-off voice or two, a bell ringing thinly and softly as if under a sheet of ice—had the same slightly abstracted quality, as if removed by one degree from actuality—as if everything in the world had been insulated by snow. But when at last, pleased, he opened his eyes, and turned them towards the window, to see for himself this long-desired and now so clearly imagined miracle—what he saw instead was brilliant sunlight on a roof; and when, astonished, he jumped out of bed and stared down into the street, expecting to see the cobbles obliterated by the snow, he saw nothing but the bare bright cobbles themselves.

Queer, the effect this extraordinary surprise had had upon him—all the following morning he had kept with him a sense as of snow falling about him, a secret screen of new snow between himself and the world. If he had not dreamed such a thing—and how could he have dreamed it while awake?—how else could one explain it? In any case, the delusion had been so vivid as to affect his entire behaviour.

He could not now remember whether it was on the first or the second morning—or was it even the third?—that his mother had drawn attention to some oddness in his manner.

'But, my darling'—she had said at the breakfast table—'what has come over you? You don't seem to be listening....'

And how often that very thing had happened since!

(Miss Buell was now asking if anyone knew the difference between the North Pole and the Magnetic Pole. Deirdre was holding up her flickering brown hand, and he could see the four white dimples that marked the knuckles.)

Perhaps it hadn't been either the second or third morning —or even the fourth or fifth. How could he be sure? How could he be sure just when the delicious *progress* had become clear? Just when it had really *begun*? The intervals weren't very precise. . . . All he now knew was, that at some point or other—perhaps the second day, perhaps the sixth—he had noticed that the presence of the snow was a little more insistent, the sound of it clearer; and, conversely, the sound of the postman's footsteps more indistinct. Not only could he not hear the steps come round the corner, he could not even hear them at the first house. It was below the first house that he heard them; and then, a few days later, it was below the second house that he heard them; and a few days later again, below the third. Gradually, gradually, the snow was becoming heavier, the sound of its seething louder, the cobblestones more and more muffled. When he found, each morning, on going to the window, after the ritual of listening, that the roofs and cobbles were as bare as ever, it made no difference. This was, after all, only what he had expected. It was even what pleased him, what rewarded him: the thing was his own, belonged to no one else. No one else knew about it, not even his mother and father. There, outside, were the bare cobbles; and here, inside, was the snow. Snow growing heavier each day, muffling the world, hiding the ugly, and deadening increasingly—above all—the steps of the postman.

'But, my darling'—she had said at the luncheon table—'what has come over you? You don't seem to listen when people speak to you. That's the third time I've asked you to pass your plate. . . .'

How was one to explain this to Mother? or to Father? There was, of course, nothing to be done about it: nothing. All one could do was to laugh embarrassedly, pretend to be a little ashamed, apologise, and take a sudden and somewhat disingenuous interest in what was being done or said. The cat had stayed out all night. He had a curious swelling on his left cheek—perhaps somebody had kicked him, or a stone had struck him. Mrs Kempton was or was not coming to tea. The house was going to be house cleaned, or 'turned out', on Wednesday instead of Friday. A new lamp was provided for his evening work—perhaps it was eyestrain which accounted for this new and so peculiar vagueness of his—Mother was looking at him with amusement as she said this, but with something else as well. A new lamp? A new lamp. Yes Mother, No Mother, Yes Mother. School is going very well. The geometry is very easy. The history is very dull. The geography is very interesting—particularly when it takes one to the North Pole. Why the North Pole? Oh, well, it would be fun to be an explorer. Another Peary or Scott or Shackleton. And then abruptly he found his interest in the talk at an end, stared at the pudding on his plate, listened, waited, and began once more—ah, how heavenly, too, the first beginnings—to hear or feel—for could he actually hear it?—the silent snow, the secret snow.

(Miss Buell was telling them about the search for the Northwest Passage, about Hendrik Hudson, the *Half Moon*.)

This had been, indeed, the only distressing feature of the new experience: the fact that it so increasingly had brought him into a kind of mute misunderstanding, or even conflict, with his father and mother. It was as if he were trying to lead a double life. On the one hand he had to be Paul Hasleman, and keep up the appearance of being that person—dress, wash, and answer intelligently when spoken to; on the other, he had to explore this new world which had been opened to him. Nor could there be the slightest doubt—not the slightest—that the new world was the profounder and more wonderful of the two. It was irresistible. It was miraculous. Its beauty was simply beyond anything —beyond speech as beyond thought—utterly incommunicable. But how then, between the two worlds, of which he was thus constantly aware, was he to keep a balance? One must get up, one must go to breakfast, one must talk with Mother, go to school, do one's lessons—and, in all this, try not to appear too much of a fool. But if all the while one was also trying to extract the full deliciousness of another and quite separate existence, one which could not easily (if at all) be spoken of—how was one to manage? How was one to explain? Would it be safe to explain? Would it be absurd? Would it merely mean that he would get into some obscure kind of trouble?

These thoughts came and went, came and went, as softly and secretly as the snow; they were not precisely a disturbance, perhaps they were even a pleasure; he liked to have them; their presence was something almost palpable, something he could stroke with his hand, without closing his eyes, and without ceasing to see Miss Buell and the schoolroom and the globe and the freckles on Deirdre's neck; nevertheless he did in a sense cease to see, or to see the obvious external world, and substituted for this vision the vision of snow, the sound of snow, and the slow, almost soundless, approach of the postman. Yesterday, it had been only at the sixth house that the postman had become audible; the snow was much deeper now, it was falling more swiftly and heavily, the sound of its seething was more distinct, more soothing, more persistent. And this morning, it had been— as nearly as he could figure—just above the seventh house —perhaps only a step or two above: at most, he had heard two or three footsteps before the knock had sounded. . . . And with each such narrowing of the sphere, each nearer approach of the limit at which the postman was first audible, it was odd how sharply was increased the amount of illusion which had to be carried into the ordinary business of daily life. Each day it was harder to get out of bed, to go to the window, to look out at the—as always—perfectly empty and snowless street. Each day it was more difficult to go through the perfunctory motions of greeting Mother and Father at breakfast, to reply to their questions, to put his books together and go to school. And at school, how extraordinarily hard to conduct with success simultaneously the public life and the life that was secret. There were times when he longed—positively ached—to tell everyone about it—to burst out with it—only to be checked almost at once by a far-off feeling as of some faint absurdity which was inherent in it—but *was* it absurd?—and more importantly by a sense of mysterious power in his very secrecy. Yes: it must be kept secret. That, more and more, became clear. At whatever cost to himself, whatever pain to others—

(Miss Buell looked straight at him, smiling, and said, 'Perhaps we'll ask Paul. I'm sure Paul will come out of his day-dream long enough to be able to tell us. Won't you, Paul?' He rose slowly from his chair, resting one hand on the brightly varnished desk, and deliberately stared through the snow towards the blackboard. It was an effort, but it was amusing to make it. 'Yes,' he said slowly, 'it was what we now call the Hudson River. This he thought to be the Northwest Passage. He was disappointed.' He sat down again, and as he did so Deirdre half turned in the chair and gave him a shy smile, of approval and admiration.

At whatever pain to others.

This part of it was very puzzling, very puzzling. Mother was very nice, and so was Father. Yes, that was all true enough. He wanted to be nice to them, to tell them everything—and yet, was it really wrong of him to want to have a secret place of his own?

At bedtime, the night before, Mother had said, 'If this goes on, my lad, we'll have to see a doctor, we will! We can't have our boy—' But what was it she had said? 'Live in another world'? 'Live so far away'? The word 'far' had been in it, he was sure, and then Mother had taken up a magazine again and laughed a little, but with an expression which wasn't mirthful. He had felt sorry for her. . . .

The bell rang for dismissal. The sound came to him through long curved parallels of falling snow. He saw Deirdre rise, and had himself risen almost as soon—but not quite as soon—as she.

II

On the walk homeward, which was timeless, it pleased him to see through the accompaniment, or counterpoint, of snow, the items of mere externality on his way. There were many kinds of bricks in the pavements, and laid in many kinds of pattern. The garden walls too were various, some of wooden palings, some of plaster, some of stone. Twigs of bushes leaned over the walls; the little hard green winter-buds of lilac, on grey stems, sheathed and fat; other branches very thin and fine and black and desiccated. Dirty sparrows huddled in the bushes, as dull in colour as dead fruit left in leafless trees. A single starling creaked on a weather vane. In the gutter, beside a drain, was a scrap of torn and dirty newspaper, caught in a little delta of filth; the word ECZEMA appeared in large capitals, and below it was a letter from Mrs Amelia D. Cravath, 2100 Pine Street, Fort Worth, Texas, to the effect that after being a sufferer for years she had been cured by Caley's Ointment. In the little delta, beside the fan-shaped and deeply runnelled continent of brown mud, were lost twigs, descended from their parent trees, dead matches, a rusty horse-chestnut burr, a small concentration of sparkling gravel on the lip of the sewer, a fragment of eggshell, a streak of yellow sawdust which had been wet and was now dry and congealed, a brown pebble, and a broken feather. Further on was a cement pavement, ruled into geometrical parallelograms, with a brass inlay at one end commemorating the contractors who had laid it, and, halfway across, an irregular and random series of dog-tracks, immortalised in synthetic stone. He knew these well, and always stepped on them; to cover the little hollows with his own foot had always been a queer pleasure; today he did it once more, but perfunctorily and detachedly, all the while thinking of something else. That was a dog, a long time ago, who had made a mistake and walked on the cement while it was still wet. He had probably wagged his tail, but that hadn't been recorded. Now, Paul Hasleman, aged twelve, on his way home from school, crossed the same river, which in the meantime had frozen into rock. Homeward through the snow, the snow falling in bright sunshine. Homeward?

Then came the gateway with the two posts surmounted by egg-shaped stones which had been cunningly balanced on their ends, as if by Columbus, and mortared in the very act of balance: a source of perpetual wonder. On the brick wall just beyond, the letter H had been stencilled, presumably for some purpose. H? H.

The green hydrant, with a little green-painted chain attached to the brass screw-cap.

The elm tree, with the great grey wound in the bark, kidney-shaped, into which he always put his hand—to feel the cold but living wood. The injury, he had been sure, was due to the gnawings of a tethered horse. But now it deserved only a passing palm, a merely tolerant eye. There were more important things. Miracles. Beyond the thoughts of trees, mere elms. Beyond the thought of pavements, mere stone, mere brick, mere cement. Beyond the thoughts even of his own shoes, which trod these pavements obediently, bearing a burden—far above—of elaborate mystery. He watched them. They were not very well polished; he had neglected them, for a very good reason: they were one of the many parts of the increasing difficulty of the daily return to daily life, the morning struggle. To get up, having at last opened one's eyes, to go to the window, and discover no snow, to wash, to dress, to descend the curving stairs to breakfast—

At whatever pain to others, nevertheless, one must

persevere in severance, since the incommunicability of the experience demanded it. It was desirable of course to be kind to Mother and Father, especially as they seemed to be worried, but it was also desirable to be resolute. If they should decide—as appeared likely—to consult the doctor, Doctor Howells, and have Paul inspected, his heart listened to through a kind of dictaphone, his lungs, his stomach— well, that was all right. He would go through with it. He would give them answer for question, too—perhaps such answers as they hadn't expected? No. That would never do. For the secret world must, at all costs, be preserved.

The bird-house in the apple-tree was empty—it was the wrong time of year for wrens. The little round black door had lost its pleasure. The wrens were enjoying other houses, other nests, remoter trees. But this too was a notion which he only vaguely and grazingly entertained—as if, for the moment, he merely touched an edge of it; there was something further on, which was already assuming a sharper importance; something which already teased at the corners of his eyes, teasing also at the corner of his mind. It was funny to think that he so wanted this, so awaited it—and yet found himself enjoying this momentary dalliance with the bird-house, as if for a quite deliberate postponement and enhancement of the approaching pleasure. He was aware of his delay, of his smiling and detached and now almost uncomprehending gaze at the little bird-house; he knew what he was going to look at next: it was his own little cobbled hill-street, his own house, the little river at the bottom of the hill, the grocer's shop with the cardboard man in the window—and now, thinking of all this, he turned his head, still smiling, and looking quickly right and left through the snow-laden sunlight.

And the mist of snow, as he had foreseen, was still on it —a ghost of snow falling in the bright sunlight, softly and steadily floating and turning and pausing, soundlessly meeting the snow that covered, as with a transparent mirage, the bare bright cobbles. He loved it—he stood still and loved it. Its beauty was paralysing—beyond all words, all experience, all dream. No fairy-story he had ever read could be compared with it—none had ever given him this extraordinary combination of ethereal loveliness with a something else, unnameable, which was just faintly and deliciously terrifying. What was this thing? As he thought of it, he looked upward towards his own bedroom window, which was open—and it was as if he looked straight into the room and saw himself lying half awake in his bed. There he was —at this very instant he was still perhaps actually there— more truly there than standing here at the edge of the cobbled hill-street, with one hand lifted to shade his eyes against the snow-sun. Had he indeed ever left his room, in all this time? since that very first morning? Was the whole progress still being enacted there, was it still the same morning, and himself not yet wholly awake? And even now, had the postman not yet come round the corner? . . .

This idea amused him, and automatically, as he thought of it, he turned his head and looked towards the top of the hill. There was, of course, nothing there—nothing and no one. The street was empty and quiet. And all the more because of its emptiness it occurred to him to count the houses—a thing which, oddly enough, he hadn't before thought of doing. Of course, he had known there weren't many—many, that is, on his own side of the street, which were the ones that figured in the postman's progress—but nevertheless it came to him as something of a shock to find that there were precisely *six*, above his own house—his own house was the seventh.

Six!

Astonished, he looked at his own house—looked at the door, on which was the number thirteen—and then realised that the whole thing was exactly and logically and absurdly what he ought to have known. Just the same, the realisation gave him abruptly, and even a little frighteningly, a sense of hurry. He was being hurried—he was being rushed. For —he knit his brows—he couldn't be mistaken—it was just above the *seventh* house, his *own* house, that the postman had first been audible this very morning. But in that case—in that case—did it mean that tomorrow he would hear nothing? The knock he had heard must have been the knock of their own door. Did it mean—and this was an idea which gave him a really extraordinary feeling of surprise—that he would never hear the postman again?—that tomorrow morning the postman would already have passed the house, in a snow by then so deep as to render his footsteps completely inaudible? That he would have made his approach down the snow-filled street so soundlessly, so secretly, that he, Paul Hasleman, there lying in bed, would not have woken in time, or waking, would have heard nothing?

But how could that be? Unless even the knocker should be muffled in the snow—frozen tight, perhaps? . . . But in that case—

A vague feeling of disappointment came over him; a vague sadness, as if he felt himself deprived of something which he had long looked forward to, something much prized. After all this, all this beautiful progress, the slow delicious advance of the postman through the silent and secret snow, the knock creeping closer each day, and the footsteps nearer, the audible compass of the world thus daily narrowed, narrowed, narrowed, as the snow soothingly and beautifully encroached and deepened, after all this, was he to be defrauded of the one thing he had so wanted—to be able to count, as it were, the last two or three solemn footsteps, as they finally approached his own door? Was it all going to happen, at the end, so suddenly? Or indeed, had it already happened? With no slow and subtle gradations of menace, in which he could luxuriate?

He gazed upward again, towards his own window which flashed in the sun: and this time almost with a feeling that it would be better if he *were* still in bed, in that room; for in that case this must still be the first morning, and there would be six more mornings to come—or, for that matter, seven or eight or nine—how could he be sure?—or even more.

III

After supper, the inquisition began. He stood before the doctor, under the lamp, and submitted silently to the usual thumpings and tappings.

'Now will you please say "Ah!"?'

'Ah!'

'Now again please, if you don't mind.'

'Ah.'

'Say it slowly and hold it if you can—'

'Ah-h-h-h-h-h—'

'Good.'

How silly all this was. As if it had anything to do with his throat! Or his heart or lungs!

Relaxing his mouth, of which the corners, after all this absurd stretching, felt uncomfortable, he avoided the doctor's eyes, and stared towards the fireplace, past his mother's feet (in grey slippers) which projected from the green chair, and his father's feet (in brown slippers) which stood neatly side by side on the hearth-rug.

'Hm. There is certainly nothing wrong there . . .'

He felt the doctor's eyes fixed upon him, and, as if merely to be polite, returned the look, but with a feeling of justifiable evasiveness.

'Now, young man, tell me—do you feel all right?'

'Yes, sir, quite all right.'

'No headaches? No dizziness?'

'No, I don't think so.'

'Let me see. Let's get a book, if you don't mind—yes, thank you, that will do splendidly—and now, Paul, if you'll just read it, holding it as you would normally hold it—'

He took the book and read:

'And another praise have I to tell for this the city our mother, the gift of a great god, a glory of the land most high; the might of horses, the might of young horses, the might of the sea. . . . For thou, son of Cronus, our lord Poseidon, hast throned herein this pride, since in these roads first thou didst show forth the curb that cures the rage of steeds. And the shapely oar, apt to men's hands, hath a wonderous speed on the brine, following the hundred-footed Nereids. . . . O land that art praised above all lands, now is it for thee to make those bright praises seen in deeds.'

He stopped, tentatively, and lowered the heavy book.

'No—as I thought—there is certainly no superficial sign of eyestrain.'

Silence thronged the room, and he was aware of the focused scrutiny of the three people who confronted him. . . .

'We could have his eyes examined—but I believe it is something else.'

'What could it be?' This was his father's voice.

'It's only this curious absent-minded—' This was his mother's voice.

In the presence of the doctor, they both seemed irritatingly apologetic.

'I believe it is something else. Now, Paul—I would like very much to ask you a question or two. You will answer them, won't you—you know I'm an old, old friend of yours, eh? That's right! . . .'

His back was thumped twice by the doctor's fat fist—then the doctor was grinning at him with false amiability, while with one finger-nail he was scratching the top button of his waistcoat. Beyond the doctor's shoulder was the fire, the fingers of flame making light prestidigitation against the sooty fireback, the soft sound of their random flutter the only sound.

'I would like to know—is there anything that worries you?'

The doctor was again smiling, his eyelids low against the little black pupils, in each of which was a tiny white bead of light. Why answer him? Why answer him at all? 'At whatever pain to others'—but it was all a nuisance, this necessity for resistance, this necessity for attention: it was as if one had been stood up on a brilliantly lighted stage, under a great round blaze of spotlight; as if one were merely a trained seal, or a performing dog, or a fish, dipped out of an aquarium and held up by the tail. It would serve them right if he were merely to bark or growl. And meanwhile, to miss these last few precious hours, these hours of which every minute was more beautiful than the last, more menacing—? He still looked, as if from a great distance, at the beads of light in the doctor's eyes, at the fixed false smile, and then, beyond, once more at his mother's slippers, his father's slippers, the soft flutter of the fire. Even here, even amongst these hostile presences, and in this arranged light, he could see the snow, he could hear it—it was in the corners of the room, where the shadow was deepest, under the sofa, behind the half-opened door which led to the dining room. It was gentler here, softer, its seethe the quietest of whispers, as if, in deference to a drawing-room, it had quite deliberately put on its 'manners'; it kept itself out of sight, obliterated itself, but distinctly with an air of saying, 'Ah, but just wait! Wait till we are alone together! Then I will begin to tell you something new! Something white! something cold! something sleepy! something of cease, and peace, and the long bright curve of space! Tell them to go away. Banish them. Refuse to speak. Leave them, go upstairs to your room, turn out the light and get into bed—I will go with you, I will be waiting for you, I will tell you a better story than Little Kay of the Skates, or the Snow Ghost—I will surround your bed, I will close the windows, pile a deep drift against the door, so that none will ever again be able to enter. Speak to them! . . .' It seemed as if the little hissing voice came from a slow white spiral of falling flakes in the corner by the front window—but he could not be sure. He felt himself smiling, then, and said to the doctor, but without looking at him, looking beyond him still—

'Oh, no, I think not—'

'But are you sure, my boy?'

His father's voice came softly and coldly then—the familiar voice of silken warning. . . .

'You needn't answer at once, Paul—remember we're trying to help you—think it over and be quite sure, won't you?'

He felt himself smiling again, at the notion of being quite sure. What a joke! As if he weren't so sure that reassurance was no longer necessary, and all this cross-examination a ridiculous farce, a grotesque parody! What could they know about it? These gross intelligences, these humdrum minds so bound to the usual, the ordinary? Impossible to tell them about it! Why, even now, even now, with the proof so abundant, so formidable, so imminent, so appallingly present here in this very room, could they believe it?—could even his mother believe it? No—it was only too plain that if anything were said about it, the merest hint given, they would be incredulous—they would laugh—they would say 'Absurd!'—think things about him which weren't true. . . .

'Why no, I'm not worried—why should I be?'

He looked then straight at the doctor's low-lidded eyes, looked from one of them to the other, from one bead of light to the other, and gave a little laugh.

The doctor seemed to be disconcerted by this. He drew back in his chair, resting a fat white hand on either knee. The smile faded slowly from his face.

'Well, Paul!' he said, and paused gravely, 'I'm afraid you don't take this quite seriously enough. I think you perhaps don't quite realise—don't quite realise—' He took a deep quick breath, and turned, as if helpless, at a loss for words, to the others. But Mother and Father were both silent—no help was forthcoming.

'You must surely know, be aware, that you have not been quite yourself, of late? Don't you know that? . . .'

It was amusing to watch the doctor's renewed attempt at a smile, a queer disorganised look, as of confidential embarrassment.

'I feel all right, sir,' he said, and again gave the little laugh.

'And we're trying to help you.' The doctor's tone sharpened.

'Yes, sir, I know. But why? I'm all right. I'm just *thinking*, that's all.'

His mother made a quick movement forward, resting a hand on the back of the doctor's chair.

'Thinking?' she said. 'But my dear, about what?'

This was a direct challenge—and would have to be directly met. But before he met it, he looked again into the corner by the door, as if for reassurance. He smiled again at what he saw, at what he heard. The little spiral was still there, still softly whirling, like the ghost of a white kitten chasing the ghost of a white tail, and making as it did the faintest of whispers. It was all right! If only he could remain firm, everything was going to be all right.

'Oh, about anything, about nothing—*you* know the way you do!'

'You mean—day-dreaming?'

'Oh, no—thinking!'

'But thinking about *what*?'

'Anything.'

He laughed a third time—but this time, happening to glance upward towards his mother's face, he was appalled at the effect his laughter seemed to have upon her. Her mouth had opened in an expression of horror. . . . This was too bad! Unfortunate! He had known it would cause pain, of course—but he hadn't expected it to be quite so bad as this. Perhaps—perhaps if he just gave them a tiny gleaming hint—?

'About the snow,' he said.

'What on earth!' This was his father's voice. The brown slippers came a step nearer on the hearth-rug.

'But my dear, what do you mean!' This was his mother's voice.

The doctor merely stared.

'Just *snow*, that's all. I like to think about it.'

'Tell us about it, my boy.'

'But that's all it is. There's nothing to tell. *You* know what snow is.'

This he said almost angrily, for he felt that they were trying to corner him. He turned sideways so as no longer to face the doctor, and the better to see the inch of blackness between the window-sill and the lowered curtains,—the cold inch of beckoning and delicious night. At once he felt better, more assured.

'Mother—can I go to bed, now, please? I've got a headache.'

'But I thought you said—'

'It's just come. It's all these questions—! Can I, Mother?'

'You can go as soon as the doctor has finished.'

'Don't you think this thing ought to be gone into thoroughly, and *now*?' This was Father's voice. The brown slippers again came a step nearer, the voice was the well-known 'punishment' voice, resonant and cruel.

'Oh, what's the use, Norman—'

Quite suddenly, everyone was silent. And without precisely facing them, nevertheless he was aware that all three of them were watching him with an extraordinary intensity—staring hard at him—as if he had done something monstrous, or was himself some kind of monster. He could hear the soft irregular flutter of the flames; the cluck-click-cluck-click of the clock; far and faint, two sudden spurts of laughter from the kitchen, as quickly cut off as begun; a murmur of water in the pipes; and then, the silence seemed to deepen, to spread out, to become worldlong and worldwide, to become timeless and shapeless, and to centre inevitably and rightly, with a slow and sleepy but enormous concentration of all power, on the beginning of a new sound. What this new sound was going to be, he knew perfectly well. It might begin with a hiss, but it would end with a roar—there was no time to lose—he must escape. It mustn't happen here—

Without another word, he turned and ran up the stairs.

IV

Not a moment too soon. The darkness was coming in long white waves. A prolonged sibilance filled the night—a great seamless seethe of wild influence went abruptly across it—a cold low humming shook the windows. He shut the door and flung off his clothes in the dark. The bare black floor was like a raft tossed in waves of snow, almost overwhelmed, washed under whitely, up again, smothered in curled billows of feather. The snow was laughing: it spoke from all sides at once: it pressed closer to him as he ran and jumped exulting into his bed.

'Listen to us!' it said. 'Listen! We have come to tell you the story we told you about. You remember? Lie down. Shut your eyes, now—you will no longer see much—in this white darkness who could see, or want to see? We will take the place of everything . . . Listen—'

A beautiful varying dance of snow began at the front of the room, came forward and then retreated, flattened out towards the floor, then rose fountain-like to the ceiling, swayed, recruited itself from a new stream of flakes which poured laughing in through the humming window, advanced again, lifted long white arms. It said peace, it said remoteness, it said cold—it said—

But then a gash of horrible light fell brutally across the room from the opening door—the snow drew back hissing—something alien had come into the room—something hostile. This thing rushed at him, clutched at him, shook him—and he was not merely horrified, he was filled with such a loathing as he had never known. What was this? this cruel disturbance? this act of anger and hate? It was as if he had to reach up a hand towards another world for any understanding of it—an effort of which he was only barely capable. But of that other world he still remembered just enough to know the exorcising words. They tore themselves from his other life suddenly—

'Mother! Mother! Go away! I hate you!'

And with that effort, everything was solved, everything became all right: the seamless hiss advanced once more, the long white wavering lines rose and fell like enormous whispering sea-waves, the whisper becoming louder, the laughter more numerous.

'Listen!' it said. 'We'll tell you the last, the most beautiful and secret story—shut your eyes—it is a very small story —a story that gets smaller and smaller—it comes inward instead of opening like a flower—it is a flower becoming a seed—a little cold seed—do you hear? We are leaning closer to you—'

The hiss was now becoming a roar—the whole world was a vast moving screen of snow—but even now it said peace, it said remoteness, it said cold, it said sleep.

Midnight Express

ALFRED NOYES

Here is a strange little gem of a tale—a mystery story about a mystery story—or a picture in a mystery novel to be precise. I suspect that like Mortimer in the story, most people have at some time come across a picture in an old book which has both un-nerved and fascinated them simultaneously. The kind of illustration that makes you feel uneasy, but you just cannot help being drawn back to it time and time again. Appropriately enough, I first came across "Midnight Express" in an old collection of horror stories which had a grinning skull on the front cover. I remember it well because the skull always looked slightly different every time your eye was drawn back to it. Or it did to me—which was just the kind of reaction Alfred Noyes had in mind when he wrote the uncanny tale which begins like this. . . .

It was a battered old book, bound in red buckram. He found it, when he was twelve years old, on an upper shelf in his father's library; and, against all the rules, he took it to his bedroom to read by candlelight, when the rest of the rambling old Elizabethan house was flooded with darkness. That was how young Mortimer always thought of it. His own room was a little isolated cell, in which, with stolen candle ends, he could keep the surrounding darkness at bay, while everyone else had surrendered to sleep and allowed the outer night to come flooding in. By contrast with those unconscious ones, his elders, it made him feel intensely alive in every nerve and fibre of his young brain. The ticking of the grandfather clock in the hall below, the beating of his own heart; the long-drawn rhythmical 'ah' of the sea on the distant coast, all filled him with a sense of overwhelming mystery; and, as he read, the soft thud of a blinded moth, striking the wall above the candle, would make him start and listen like a creature of the woods at the sound of a cracking twig.

The battered old book had the strangest fascination for him, though he never quite grasped the thread of the story. It was called *The Midnight Express*, and there was one illustration, on the fiftieth page, at which he could never bear to look. It frightened him.

Young Mortimer never understood the effect of that picture on him. He was an imaginative, but not a neurotic youngster; and he avoided the fiftieth page as he might have hurried past a dark corner on the stairs when he was six years old, or as the grown man on the lonely road, in *The Ancient Mariner*, who, having once looked round, walks on, and turns no more his head. There was nothing in the picture—apparently—to account for this haunting dread. Darkness, indeed, was almost its chief characteristic. It showed an empty railway platform—at night—lit by a single dreary lamp: an empty railway platform that suggested a deserted and lonely junction in some remote part of the country. There was only one figure on the platform: the dark figure of a man, standing almost directly under the lamp with his face turned away towards the black mouth of a tunnel which—for some strange reason—plunged the imagination of the child into a pit of horror. The man seemed to be listening. His attitude was tense, expectant, as though he were awaiting some fearful tragedy. There was nothing in the text, so far as the child read, and could understand, to account for this waking nightmare. He could neither resist the fascination of the book, nor face that picture in the stillness and loneliness of the night. He pinned it down to the page facing it with two long pins, so that he should not come upon it by accident. Then he determined to read the whole story through. But, always, before he came to page fifty, he fell asleep; and the outlines of what he had read were blurred; and the next night he had to begin again; and again, before he came to the fiftieth page, he fell asleep.

He grew up, and forgot all about the book and the picture. But halfway through his life, at that strange and critical time when Dante entered the dark wood, leaving the direct path behind him, he found himself, a little before midnight, waiting for a train at a lonely junction; and, as the station-clock began to strike twelve he remembered; remembered like a man awakening from a long dream—

There, under the single dreary lamp, on the long glimmering platform, was the dark and solitary figure that he knew. Its face was turned away from him towards the black mouth of the tunnel. It seemed to be listening, tense, expectant, just as it had been thirty-eight years ago.

But he was not frightened now, as he had been in childhood. He would go up to that solitary figure, confront it, and see the face that had so long been hidden, so long averted from him. He would walk up quietly, and make some excuse for speaking to it: he would ask it, for instance, if the train was going to be late. It should be easy for a grown man to do this; but his hands were clenched, when he took the first step, as if he, too, were tense and expectant. Quietly, but with the old vague instincts awaking, he went towards the dark figure under the lamp, passed it, swung round abruptly to speak to it; and saw—without speaking, without being able to speak—

It was himself—staring back at himself—as in some mocking mirror, his own eyes alive in his own white face, looking into his own eyes, alive—

The nerves of his heart tingled as though their own electric currents would paralyse it. A wave of panic went through him. He turned, gasped, stumbled, broke into a blind run, out through the deserted and echoing ticket-office, on to the long moonlit road behind the station. The whole countryside seemed to be utterly deserted. The moonbeams flooded it with the loneliness of their own deserted satellite.

He paused for a moment, and heard, like the echo of his own footsteps, the stumbling run of something that followed over the wooden floor within the ticket-office. Then he abandoned himself shamelessly to his fear; and ran, sweating like a terrified beast, down the long white road between the two endless lines of ghostly poplars each answering another, into what seemed an infinite distance. On one side of the road there was a long straight canal, in which one of the lines of poplars was again endlessly reflected. He heard the footsteps echoing behind him. They seemed to be slowly, but steadily, gaining upon him. A quarter of a mile away, he saw a small white cottage by the roadside, a white cottage with two dark windows and a door that somehow suggested a human face. He thought to himself that, if he could reach it in time, he might find shelter and security—escape.

The thin implacable footsteps, echoing his own, were still some way off when he lurched, gasping, into the little porch; rattled the latch, thrust at the door, and found it locked against him. There was no bell or knocker. He pounded on the wood with his fists until his knuckles bled. The response was horribly slow. At last, he heard heavier footsteps within the cottage. Slowly they descended the creaking stair. Slowly the door was unlocked. A tall shadowy figure stood before him, holding a lighted candle, in such a way that he could see little either of the holder's face or form; but to his dumb horror there seemed to be a cerecloth wrapped round the face.

No words passed between them. The figure beckoned him in; and, as he obeyed, it locked the door behind him. Then, beckoning him again, without a word, the figure went before him up the crooked stair, with the ghostly candle casting huge and grotesque shadows on the whitewashed walls and ceiling.

They entered an upper room, in which there was a bright fire burning, with an armchair on either side of it, and a small oak table, on which there lay a battered old book, bound in dark red buckram. It seemed as though the guest had been long expected and all things were prepared.

The figure pointed to one of the armchairs, placed the candlestick on the table by the book (for there was no other light but that of the fire) and withdrew without a word, locking the door behind him.

Mortimer looked at the candlestick. It seemed familiar. The smell of the guttering wax brought back the little room in the old Elizabethan house. He picked up the book with trembling fingers. He recognised it at once, though he had long forgotten everything about the story. He remembered the ink stain on the title page; and then, with a shock of recollection, he came on the fiftieth page, which he had pinned down in childhood. The pins were still there. He touched them again—the very pins which his trembling childish fingers had used so long ago.

He turned back to the beginning. He was determined to read it to the end now, and discover what it all was about. He felt that it must all be set down there, in print; and, though in childhood he could not understand it, he would be able to fathom it now.

It was called *The Midnight Express*; and, as he read the first paragraph, it began to dawn upon him slowly, fearfully, inevitably.

It was the story of a man who, in childhood, long ago, had chanced upon a book, in which there was a picture that frightened him. He had grown up and forgotten it and one night, upon a lonely railway platform, he had found himself in the remembered scene of the picture; he had confronted the solitary figure under the lamp; recognised it, and fled in panic. He had taken shelter in a wayside cottage; had been led to an upper room, found the book awaiting him and had begun to read it right through, to the very end, at last— And this book, too, was called The Midnight Express. *And it was the story of a man who, in childhood—It would go on thus, forever and forever, and forever. There was no escape.*

But when the story came to the wayside cottage, for the third time, a deeper suspicion began to dawn upon him, slowly, fearfully, inevitably—Although there was no escape, he could at least try to grasp more clearly the details of the strange circle, the fearful wheel, in which he was moving.

There was nothing new about the details. They had been there all the time; but he had not grasped their significance. That was all. *The strange and dreadful being that had led him up the crooked stair—who and what was That?*

The story mentioned something that had escaped him. The strange host, who had given him shelter, was about his own height. Could it be that he also—and was this why the face was hidden?

At the very moment when he asked himself that question, he heard the click of the key in the locked door.

The strange host was entering—moving towards him from behind—casting a grotesque shadow, larger than human, on the white walls in the guttering candlelight.

It was there, seated on the other side of the fire, facing him. With a horrible nonchalance, as a woman might prepare to remove a veil, it raised its hands to unwind the cerecloth from its face. He knew to whom it would belong. But would it be dead or living?

There was no way out but one. As Mortimer plunged forward and seized the tormentor by the throat, his own throat was gripped with the same brutal force. The echoes of their strangled cry were indistinguishable; and when the last confused sounds died out together, the stillness of the room was so deep that you might have heard—the ticking of the old grandfather clock, and the long-drawn rhythmical 'ah' of the sea, on a distant coast, thirty-eight years ago.

But Mortimer had escaped at last. Perhaps, after all he had caught the midnight express.

It was a battered old book, bound in red buckram . . .

The October Game

RAY BRADBURY

Now, sadly on my part, we have almost reached the end of the book, although there are quite a number more suitable stories that I could well have included. To close, though, I have specially picked a story about the one night of the year when all the denizens of darkness are said to be abroad, Halloween. By tradition, this night, October 31st —the last night of summer—is the time when the spirits of the dead rise from their graves and mingle with witches and demons for a last fling before winter sets in. Although it is now regarded as rather a festive occasion for dressing up and playing tricks on each other, the celebration was once taken far more seriously. In the past our ancestors paid homage to the spirits of the dead by lighting great fires around which they danced, and in doing so supposedly comforted the departed and provided them with enough warmth to see them through the long, cold winter ahead. Today, in these less superstitious times, we find such ideas a little hard to accept—and so make a game out of the whole thing. But games can go wrong in even the most ordered society as our last skilful contributor, Ray Bradbury, sets out to prove. The bump you will experience in your imagination as you reach the last page of this story will, I am sure, be matched only by the bumping of your heart . . .

He put the gun back into the bureau drawer and shut the drawer.

No, not that way. Louise wouldn't suffer that way. She would be dead and it would be over and she wouldn't suffer. It was very important that this thing have, above all, duration. Duration through imagination. How to prolong the suffering? How, first of all, to bring it about? Well.

The man standing before the bedroom mirror carefully fitted his cuff links together. He paused long enough to hear the children run by swiftly on the street below, outside this warm two-storey house; like so many grey mice the children, like so many leaves.

By the sound of the children you knew the calendar day. By their screams you knew what evening it was. You knew it was very late in the year. October. The last day of October, with white bone masks and cut pumpkins and the smell of dropped candle fat.

No. Things hadn't been right for some time. October didn't help any. If anything it made things worse. He adjusted his black bow-tie. If this were spring, he nodded slowly, quietly, emotionlessly, at his image in the mirror, then there might be a chance. But tonight all the world was burning down into ruin. There was no green of spring, none of the freshness, none of the promise.

There was a soft running in the hall. 'That's Marion,' he told himself. 'My little one. All eight quiet years of her. Never a word. Just her luminous grey eyes and her wondering little mouth.' His daughter had been in and out all evening, trying on various masks, asking him which was most terrifying, most horrible. They had both finally decided on the skeleton mask. It was 'just awful!' It would 'scare the beans' from people!

Again he caught the long look of thought and deliberation he gave himself in the mirror. He had never liked October. Ever since he first lay in the autumn leaves before his grandmother's house many years ago and heard the wind and saw the empty trees. It had made him cry, without a reason. And a little of that sadness returned each year to him. It always went away with spring.

But, it was different tonight. There was a feeling of autumn coming to last a million years.

There would be no spring.

He had been crying quietly all evening. It did not show, not a vestige of it, on his face. It was all somewhere hidden, but it wouldn't stop.

A rich syrupy smell of sweets filled the bustling house. Louise had laid out apples in new skins of caramel, there were vast bowls of punch fresh mixed, stringed apples in each door, scooped, vented pumpkins peering triangularly from each cold window. There was a waiting water tub in the centre of the living-room, waiting, with a sack of apples nearby, for bobbling to begin. All that was needed was the catalyst, the inpouring of children, to start the apples bobbling, the stringed apples penduluming in the crowded doors, the sweets to vanish, the halls to echo with fright or delight, it was all the same.

Now, the house was silent with preparation. And just a little more than that.

Louise had managed to be in every other room save the room he was in today. It was her very fine way of intimating, Oh look, Mich, see how busy I am! So busy that when you walk into a room *I'm* in there's always something I need to do in *another* room! Just see how I dash about!

For a while he had played a little game with her, a nasty childish game. When she was in the kitchen then he came to the kitchen, saying, 'I need a glass of water.' After a moment, him standing, drinking water, she like a crystal witch over the caramel brew bubbling like a prehistoric mudpot on the stove, she said, 'Oh, I must light the window pumpkins!' and she rushed to the living-room to make the pumpkins smile with light. He came after her, smiling, 'I must get my pipe.' 'Oh, the cider!' she had cried, running to the dining-room. 'I'll check the cider,' he had said. But when he tried following she ran to the bathroom and locked the door.

He stood outside the bathroom door, laughing strangely and senselessly, his pipe gone cold in his mouth, and then, tired of the game, but stubborn, he waited another five minutes. There was not a sound from the bath. And lest she enjoy in any way knowing that he waited outside, irritated, he suddenly jerked about and walked upstairs, whistling merrily.

At the top of the stairs he had waited. Finally he had heard the bathroom door unlatch and she had come out and life below-stairs had resumed, as life in a jungle must resume once a terror has passed on away and the antelope return to their spring.

Now, as he finished his bow-tie and put on his dark coat there was a mouse-rustle in the hall. Marion appeared in the door, all skeletonous in her disguise.

'How do I look, Papa?'

'Fine!'

From under the mask, blonde hair showed. From the skull sockets small blue eyes smiled. He sighed. Marion and Louise, the two silent denouncers of his virility, his dark power. What alchemy had there been in Louise that took the dark of a dark man and bleached and bleached the dark brown eyes and black black hair and washed and bleached the ingrown baby all during the period before birth until the child was born, Marion, blonde, blue-eyed, ruddy-cheeked? Sometimes he suspected that Louise had conceived the child as an idea, completely asexual, an immaculate conception of contemptuous mind and cell. As a firm rebuke to him she had produced a child in her *own* image, and, to top it, she had somehow *fixed* the doctor so he shook his head and said, 'Sorry, Mr Wilder, your wife will never have another child. This is the *last* one.'

'And I wanted a boy,' Mich had said, eight years ago.

He almost bent to take hold of Marion now, in her skull mask. He felt an inexplicable rush of pity for her, because she had never had a father's love, only the crushing, holding love of a loveless mother. But most of all he pitied himself, that somehow he had not made the most of a bad birth, enjoyed his daughter for herself, regardless of her not being dark and a son and like himself. Somewhere he had missed out. Other things being equal, he would have loved the child. But Louise hadn't wanted a child, anyway, in the first place. She had been frightened of the idea of birth. He had forced the child on her, and from that night, all through the year until the agony of the birth itself, Louise had lived in another part of the house. She had expected to die with the forced child. It had been very easy for Louise to hate this husband who so wanted a son that he gave his only wife over to the mortuary.

But—Louise had lived. And in triumph! Her eyes, the day he came to the hospital, were cold. I'm alive, they said. And I have a *blonde* daughter! Just look! And when he had put out a hand to touch, the mother had turned away to conspire with her new pink daughter-child—away from that dark forcing murderer. It had all been so beautifully ironic. His selfishness deserved it.

But now it was October again. There had been other Octobers and when he thought of the long winter he had been filled with horror year after year to think of the endless months mortared into the house by an insane fall of snow, trapped with a woman and child, neither of whom loved him, for months on end. During the eight years there had been respites. In spring and summer you got out, walked, picnicked; these were desperate solutions to the desperate problem of a hated man.

But, in winter, the hikes and picnics and escapes fell away with the leaves. Life, like a tree, stood empty, the fruit picked, the sap run to earth. Yes, you invited people in, but people were hard to get in winter with blizzards and all. Once he had been clever enough to save for a Florida trip. They had gone south. He had walked in the open.

But now, the eighth winter coming, he knew things were finally at an end. He simply could not wear this one through. There was an acid walled off in him that slowly had eaten through tissue and tissue over the years, and now, tonight, it would reach the wild explosive in him and all would be over!

There was a mad ringing of the bell below. In the hall, Louise went to see. Marion, without a word, ran down to greet the first arrivals. There were shouts and hilarity.

He walked to the top of the stairs.

Louise was below, taking wraps. She was tall and slender and blonde to the point of whiteness, laughing down upon the new children.

He hesitated. What was all this? The years? The boredom

of living? Where had it gone wrong? Certainly not with the birth of the child alone. But it had been a symbol of all their tensions, he imagined. His jealousies and his business failures and all the rotten rest of it. Why didn't he just turn, pack a suitcase, and leave? No. Not without hurting Louise as much as she had hurt him. It was simple as that. Divorce wouldn't hurt her at all. It would simply be an end to numb indecision. If he thought divorce would give her pleasure in any way he would stay married the rest of his life to her, for damned spite. No, he must hurt her. Figure some way, perhaps, to take Marion away from her, legally. Yes. That was it. That would hurt most of all. To take Marion away.

'Hello down there!' He descended the stairs, beaming.

Louise didn't look up.

'Hi, Mr Wilder!'

The children shouted, waved, as he came down.

By ten o'clock the doorbell had stopped ringing, the apples were bitten from stringed doors, the pink child faces were wiped dry from the apple bobbling, napkins were smeared with caramel and punch, and he, the husband, with pleasant efficiency had taken over. He took the party right out of Louise's hands. He ran about talking to the twenty children and the twelve parents who had come and were happy with the special spiked cider he had fixed them. He supervised PIN THE TAIL ON THE DONKEY, SPIN THE BOTTLE, MUSICAL CHAIRS, and all the rest, midst fits of shouting laughter. Then, in the triangular-eyed pumpkin shine, all house lights out, he cried, 'Hush! Follow me!' he said, tiptoeing towards the cellar.

The parents, on the outer periphery of the costumed riot, commented to each other, nodding at the clever husband, speaking to the lucky wife. How *well* he got on with children, they said.

The children crowded after the husband, squealing.

'The cellar!' he cried. 'The tomb of the witch!'

More squealing. He made a mock shiver. 'Abandon hope all ye who enter here!'

The parents chuckled.

One by one the children slid down a slide which Mich had fixed up from lengths of table-section, into the dark cellar. He hissed and shouted ghastly utterances after them. A wonderful wailing filled the dark pumpkin-lighted house. Everybody talked at once. Everybody but Marion. She had gone through all the party with a minimum of sound or talk; it was all inside her, all the excitement and joy. What a little troll, he thought. With a shut mouth and shiny eyes she had watched her own party, like so many serpentines, thrown before her.

Now, the parents. With laughing reluctance they slid down the short incline, uproarious, while little Marion stood by, always wanting to see it all, to be last. Louise went down without his help. He moved to aid her, but she was gone even before he bent.

The upper house was empty and silent in the candleshine.

Marion stood by the slide. 'Here we go,' he said, and picked her up.

They sat in a vast circle in the cellar. Warmth came from the distant bulk of the furnace. The chairs stood on a long line down each wall, twenty squealing children, twelve rustling relatives, alternately spaced, with Louise down at the far end. Mich up at this end, near the stairs. He peered but saw nothing. They had all groped to their chairs, catch-as-you-can in the blackness. The entire programme from here on was to be enacted in the dark, he as Mr Interlocutor. There was a child scampering, a smell of damp cement, and the sound of the wind out in the October stars.

'Now!' cried the husband in the dark cellar. 'Quiet!'

Everybody settled.

The room was black black. Not a light, not a shine, not a glint of an eye.

A scraping of crockery, a metal rattle.

'The witch is dead,' intoned the husband.

'Eeeeeeeeeeee,' said the children.

'The witch is dead, she has been killed, and here is the knife she was killed with.'

He handed over the knife. It was passed from hand to hand, down and round the circle, with chuckles and little odd cries and comments from the adults.

'The witch is dead, and this is her head,' whispered the husband, and handed an item to the nearest person.

'Oh, I know how this game is played,' some child cried, happily, in the dark. 'He gets some old chicken innards from the fridge and hands them around and says, "These are her innards!" And he makes a clay head and passes it for her head, and passes a soup-bone for her arm. And he takes a marble and says, "This is her eye!" And he takes some corn and says, "This is her teeth!" And he takes a sack of plum pudding and gives that and says, "This is her stomach!" I know how *this* is played!'

'Hush, you'll spoil everything,' some girl said.

'The witch came to harm, and this is her arm,' said Mich.

'Eeeee!'

The items were passed and passed, like hot potatoes, around the circle. Some children screamed, wouldn't touch them. Some ran from their chairs to stand in the centre of the cellar until the grisly items had passed.

'Aw, it's only chicken insides,' scoffed a boy. 'Come back, Helen!'

Shot from hand to hand, with small scream after scream, the items went down the line, down, down, to be followed by another and another.

'The witch cut apart, and this is her heart,' said the husband.

Six or seven items moving at once through the laughing, trembling dark.

Louise spoke up. 'Marion, don't be afraid; it's only play.'

Marion didn't say anything.

'Marion?' asked Louise. 'Are you afraid?'

Marion didn't speak.

'She's all right,' said the husband. 'She's not afraid.'

On and on the passing, the screams, the hilarity.

The autumn wind sighed about the house. And he, the husband, stood at the head of the dark cellar, intoning the words, handing out the items.

'Marion?' asked Louise again, from far across the cellar.

Everybody was talking.

'Marion?' called Louise.

Everybody quieted.

'Marion, answer me, are you afraid?'

Marion didn't answer.

The husband stood there, at the bottom of the cellar steps.

Louise called, 'Marion, are you there?'

No answer. The room was silent.

'Where's Marion?' called Louise.

'She was here,' said a boy.

'Maybe she's upstairs.'

'Marion!'

No answer. It was quiet.

Louise cried out, 'Marion, Marion!'

'Turn on the lights,' said one of the adults.

The items stopped passing. The children and adults sat with the witches' items in their hands.

'No.' Louise gasped. There was a scraping of her chair, wildly, in the dark. 'No. Don't turn on the lights, don't turn on the lights, oh God, God, God, don't turn them on, please, please *don't* turn on the lights, *don't!*' Louise was shrieking now. The entire cellar froze with the scream.

Nobody moved.

Everyone sat in the dark cellar, suspended in the suddenly frozen task of this October game; the wind blew outside, banging the house, the smell of pumpkins and apples filled the room with the smell of the objects in their fingers while one boy cried, 'I'll go upstairs and look!' and he ran upstairs hopefully and out around the house, four times around the house, calling 'Marion, Marion, Marion!' over and over and at last coming slowly down the stairs into the waiting, breathing cellar and saying to the darkness, 'I can't find her.'

Then . . . some idiot turned on the lights.

Acknowledgements

The editor is grateful to the following authors, agents and publishers for permission to reproduce copyright stories in this collection: Edward Arnold & Co for *Lost Hearts* by M. R. James; Jonathan Cape Ltd for *Nurse's Tale* by H. R. Wakefield; A. P. Watt Ltd and the Public Trustee for *The Attic* by Algernon Blackwood; Mrs Celia Keller and Arkham House Publishers for *The Thing in the Cellar* by David H. Keller; J. M. Dent and Sons Ltd for *The Dabblers* by W. F. Harvey; Joan Aiken Enterprises for *The Looking-Glass Tree* by Joan Aiken; E. J. Carnell Literary Agency for *The Human Angle* by William Tenn; A. M. Heath Ltd and Scott Meredith Literary Agency for *Sweets to the Sweet* by Robert Bloch and *Twilight Play* by August Derleth; The Author for *The Witch of Ramoth* by Mark Van Doren; The Author for *Mr Lupescu* by Anthony Boucher; A. M. Heath Ltd for *Silent Snow, Secret Snow* by Conrad Aiken; A. D. Peters Literary Agency for *The October Game* by Ray Bradbury. While every care has been taken to establish the copyright holder of material used in this anthology, in the case of any accidental infringement the editor should be contacted in care of the publishers.